Cinnamon Girl

xpecting To Fly

Cathy Hopkins is the author of the incredibly successful *Mates, Dates* and *Truth, Dare* books, as well as the highly acclaimed *Cinnamon Girl* series. She lives in North London with her husband and cats.

Cathy spends most of her time locked in a shed at the bottom of the garden pretending to write books, but she is actually in there listening to music, hippie dancing and talking to her friends on email.

Apart from that, Cathy has joined the gym and spends more time than is good for her making up excuses as to why she hasn't got time to go.

Find out more about Cathy and her books at
www.cathyhopkins.com

Cathy Hopkins

Cinnamon Girl

Expecting To Fly

PICCADILLY PRESS * LONDON

Thanks, as always, to Brenda Gardner, Anne Clark,
Melissa Hyder and all the fab team at Piccadilly
who have made working on this
and all my books a pleasure.

First published in Great Britain in 2009
by Piccadilly Press Ltd,
5 Castle Road, London NW1 8PR
www.piccadillypress.co.uk

A catalogue record for this book is available from the British Library.

ISBN: 978 1 84812 009 9

1 3 5 7 9 10 8 6 4 2

Printed in the UK by CPI Bookmarque Ltd, Croydon, CR0 4TD
Cover design by Simon Davis
Cover illustration by Sue Hellard

Chapter 1

New Year

'Who's going to go first?' I asked.

I was sitting in the kitchen at my aunt's house with Leela, Zahrah and Brook and we were huddled around the Aga, drinking banana smoothies and writing our New Year's resolutions.

Brook held up her sheet of paper. It was blank. 'I don't make resolutions. What's the point? I only break them after a few days and then feel like I've failed and who wants to start the year on a downer?'

'That's a cop-out. It's good to identify your goals,' said Zahrah. 'Then you have something to aim for. Goals, resolutions – same thing. It's good to have a plan.'

Leela laughed. 'Oo get you, Miss Stricty Pants. I reckon you will be Prime Minister one day, Zah. So what are yours, then? Number one: take over the world. Number two: make everyone start work an hour earlier. Number three: no more weekends or holidays.' She did a mock salute.

Zahrah ignored her and glanced at her list. 'Make a study plan. Choose subjects for Sixth Form.' She looked up and poked her tongue out at Leela. 'And maybe I will go for Prime Minister. Why not? If Barack Obama can be President of America, I could be Prime Minister here in the UK.'

'Boring,' groaned Brook. 'What about you, India Jane?'

I looked at my paper. *1) Go steady with Joe. 2) Exercise more. 3) Not eat so many chocs so I can get into the jeans I got for Christmas. 4) Let Tyler know that I want to be friends, not boyfriend and girlfriend.* I hesitated. *A bit lightweight compared to Zahrah's,* I thought. Even though we had serious exams soon, I hadn't considered putting anything remotely connected with school. I covered my list with my hand so that the others couldn't read what I'd written. 'Um. Be happy. I think that's going to be my New Year resolution.'

'Good one,' said Brook. 'But what *makes* you happy? What do you want to happen this year?'

'Which brings us back to goals,' said Zahrah, causing Brook to sigh wearily.

'Joe makes me happy,' I said. 'When he came over before Christmas, I felt that he was beginning to give in to what's between us.'

2

'Falling under your spell,' said Brook and she got up and began to dance, writhe and sing some mad song. '*Witch-ee women, you got the devil in your eye-ee eyes.*'

Leela picked up Brook's glass and swished around the bit of smoothie that was left. 'Hmm. Is this what is meant by going bananas? Clearly they have a funny effect on you.'

'Yeah, I wouldn't put *Enter for Britain's Got Talent* on your list of goals,' said Zahrah with a laugh.

Brook sat down and stuck her bottom lip out.

'I would totally love it if Joe stopped resisting the commitment thing and we could be a proper couple – as in dates and phone calls and not going out with anybody else,' I said.

'So that would be you and Zahrah with proper boyfriends,' said Leela. 'That leaves Brook and I as singletons. Maybe we should put that on our list. *Get boyfriend.*'

'You can't put that down like it's on a shopping list. Like – *buy shampoo, get boyfriend,*' said Zahrah.

'Why not?' asked Brook. 'You're the one who said we should have goals.'

'Not that kind of goal,' said Zahrah. 'I meant where do you want to go? Who do you want to be?'

'Where do I want to go? On a date. Who do I want to be? Someone's girlfriend. Oh chill, Zahrah,' said Brook. 'We're back at school tomorrow. Let's think about that sort of thing then.'

'Just because you don't know what you want to do,' said Zahrah.

3

'Actually I do. I want to be very very rich,' said Brook.

'You already are,' said Leela.

'We're not über-rich,' said Brook. 'I want to be very *very* rich.'

'Doesn't always happen like that. Snap your fingers, you're rich. Snap them again and you have a boyfriend. Get real, girl,' said Zahrah. 'Your head's in a cloud, as usual.'

'I have plans,' said Brook. 'Dreams. I could do design, maybe. I may write. I may marry a rich man.'

Zahrah rolled her eyes. 'And you probably will with your family connections.'

My mates couldn't be more different on the dosh scale. Brook's parents are separated but both are wealthy. Brook has always had what she wanted, being an only child between London and New York with no money spared. She lives with her mum in an elegant flat near here in Holland Park; it has tall windows, huge rooms and loads of light.

Zahrah's background is totally the opposite. Her dad's English, her mum is Ethiopian and they live in a terraced house in Queen's Park, about a quarter of the size of Brook's home and they have little money to spare.

Leela's parents are English-born Indian, both pharmacists so they are OK for money, and she is one of three with an elder brother and sister.

I have three brothers (two are my real brothers, Lewis and Dylan, and Ethan is my step-brother from Dad's first marriage). We aren't rich and we aren't poor. We live with my Aunt Sarah and

4

my cousin Kate in their fabbie-dabbie five-storey house in Holland Park. We could have been better off, but my mum and dad spent all the money they had inherited travelling the world. They're a pair of old hippies really. Luckily, my aunt invested her money wisely and now is loaded and was able to help out when Mum and Dad ran out of money and had nowhere to live. We have lived in five different countries (in the Caribbean, Italy, India, Morocco and Ireland) and I always felt I was making friends and then, just as things got comfy, I had to say goodbye, like to my best friend Erin when we left Ireland to come to London last year. To be able to stay in one place for a while has been bliss and a half and to have this bunch of mates is a dream come true. I hope Dad doesn't get it into his head to move again – to go organic farming in some remote part of Scotland or to run a painting course in Tuscany – that's just the sort of thing he thinks about from time to time. He is so restless, but both he and Mum are working at the moment and seem settled for the time being, which is great because I get to hang out with Brook, Leela and Zahrah.

The money thing rarely comes up as a problem – only sometimes, like when Brook wants to go and see a movie and the rest of us can't afford it. It's never a biggie though. We get a DVD to watch instead. Everybody's happy.

We all look very different too. I've been thinking of doing some kind of art piece featuring the four of us. Last term, the project was a self-portrait and this term we are supposed to expand the theme. I have been thinking about friends' portraits. I have an idea.

I want to call the project *Shades*. I will start with a photo of us all in profile then maybe move on to painting portraits.

I can see the first images in my mind's eye. A photo in colour and then again in black and white. It will go from Zahrah, who has the darkest skin, to Leela with her coffee-coloured skin. I will be next with my olive skin and lastly Brook with her porcelain-white complexion. I reckon I could get a whole term's work out of the different aspects of our looks. Shades of skin. Shades of hair. Textures, too. Zahrah's hair is coarse and wiry. She has it plaited in cornrows. Leela's is like silk, straight, shiny and long down her back. Mine is shoulder-length now, cut in layers, a coppery chestnut with a slight wave which I blow-dry out and Brook's is straight and so dark, it has a blue gloss in some lights. We're all brunettes yes, but the colour shines differently whether we're in the sun or in false light indoors. I was looking forward to working on the project. I'd hopefully get our different personalities in too, but I hadn't worked out how to show that in pictures yet – maybe by the way we dress. Sensible Zahrah in her jeans and T-shirts, Brook the dreamer in her pastel colours and flowers, Leela the sweetheart in her favourite pinks and me, the . . . the . . . don't know what. The Gemini. The sign of the twins, a split personality. Some days dressed in boho layers and ethnic jewellery (nicked from Mum or Aunt Sarah), some days a tomboy in jeans, Converse sneakers and boys' shirts (nicked from Lewis or Dad).

'OK, so what about you, Zahrah?' asked Brook. 'What do you want to be really?'

'Lawyer, I think. I want to make a difference. I want to be independent, that's for sure.'

'And you, Leela? You're being very quiet,' Brook said.

Leela shrugged. 'Big decision. Maybe medicine. I don't think I want to work as a pharmacist like Mum and Dad. Like you Zahrah, I'd like to make a difference. Maybe go abroad, help in a poorer country.'

I was beginning to feel inadequate. I had no idea what I wanted to do or be, never mind do anything so worthy-sounding. I hadn't given much thought to the future – to goals or careers. In the last few years, my family had moved around so much that my main concern had been settling in one place, and that goal had only been achieved so recently that I was still enjoying it too much to think about what was next.

My phone bleeped that I had a message. I picked it up from the table and glanced at the screen.

Cn U meet me? Have smthng I wnt to say. Joe X

Joe X? I thought. *Hmm. Interesting. X? What does he mean by that?* He'd never signed himself *Joe X* before. Always Joe. Just Joe. No *X*. I felt my mind go into overdrive. What could he want? Whenever we'd got close before, he'd backed off big time or given me the 'I don't do commitment' speech, sometimes before getting involved with some older pretty girl so that I got the message – he didn't do commitment with *me*. So what now? I felt my stomach turn over. I so hoped that I wasn't going to get dumped before anything had even got started.

Chapter 2

Love Is in the Air

Joe asked me to meet him in Starbucks on the High Road. Curiously, it was where I had first seen him when I came to live in London in the summer. He had been sitting in the window looking über-cool and handsome and I had put my shades on so that he wouldn't notice me looking at him, then I had snapped a photo of him to send to my mate Erin in Ireland. She had made me promise to send pics of the local talent. As I approached the café this time, there he was again, in exactly the same place and looking every bit as cute, though his hair was shorter now – it had been on his shoulders back then. I remembered thinking what great bone structure he had and how he looked thoughtful, like he'd be interesting to talk to and

8

he is. *Funny how life turns out,* I thought as I went in to join him. *Almost eight months later and he's so familiar to me now.* I felt my stomach tighten as he looked up, saw me and smiled. He'd had the same effect on me since day one. I melt inside and feel light-headed. I so hoped he wasn't going to give me the 'let's be friends' line. I'd heard that first after we'd got close in the autumn term – he'd backed off big time and given me a speech about not wanting to get involved with someone whose aunt was a friend of his mother in case it didn't work out and I got hurt blah de blah. *What now?* I asked myself. *Maybe I should come out with the 'I don't want to do commitment' line first in order to save face.*

Joe got up from the couch and leaned in to kiss me on the cheek at the moment I sat down. His lips skimmed the top of my head as I slid into my seat. 'Oops, sorry, hello,' I said and bobbed up to kiss him on the cheek, but he leaned down again at the same time and my head banged into his chin. 'Er, oops again,' I said.

Joe laughed. 'Smooth, Ruspoli.'

'That's me,' I said, as I flopped back on to the couch. 'Silver-tongued, smooth as a . . . smooth as a . . .'

'Baby's bottom?'

'Not the words I was looking for. Smooth as a —'

'Smoothie?'

'Smooth thing. Person. Type who doesn't bang heads, teeth —'

I didn't finish the sentence, because Joe leaned over, put his

9

hand firmly on the back of my neck, pulled me to him and kissed me. Properly. On the mouth. Whoa. In front of everyone. Fab. Any body part that hadn't melted before, now turned to mush. I was a mush smoothie. When we drew back to catch our breath, he grinned. 'Third time lucky.'

'Oomf,' I replied. I could always be relied on for scintillating conversation when Joe turned the charm on.

He didn't appear to notice that I had turned into a puddle. He pointed at the counter in the middle of the café. 'Drink?'

'Muh. Chocolate milkshake,' I said and groped in my pocket to find my purse.

'My treat,' said Joe and set off for the counter.

What the heckity hoola? I thought. *What's going on?* I could see two girls, Nicky and Ruby, from my year at school over at a table at the back of the café. Joe had kissed me in public – that would soon get round seeing as he is easily in the top five boy babes in the Sixth Form. As he stood in the queue, I heard a phone ring. It was his. I clearly heard him say, 'Oh hi, Mia.' He gestured to me that he was going outside to take the call. I nodded. *Now what?* I wondered. Mia was one of his exes. Why was she phoning him? And why had he gone outside to take the call? I could see him at the bus stop outside talking. He had his back turned to me so I couldn't see his expression. Was this why he had contacted me? To tell me that he was getting back together with Mia? They had dated for a while then broke up not long after term started last year. Was she calling to check that

10

he was telling me to back off or something? He glanced round to see if I was watching him. I immediately looked away. *Must look busy, cool, lalalala,* I told myself and pulled out my mobile so that I had something to do. I had a bit of money left on it so I called Erin. Luckily, she was there and I quickly filled her in on the situation. As well as being my best mate, she was good at giving advice.

'OK,' she said. 'Maintain cool. I have been reading a self-help book that my aunt Mary gave me for Christmas. It says we girls must be independent in order to be free. Not to fear solitude.'

I knew I could rely on Erin to talk some New Age gobbledegook to distract me. She chatted away while I watched Joe re-enter the café and take his place in the queue again. He looked over and gave me the thumbs-up. I nodded back like I was oh-so-busy with my phone call, too.

'Call me later with all the details,' said Erin. 'Remember, we are free. We don't need boys. We are independent free spirits.'

'Free. Independent,' I agreed, but I crossed my fingers as I said it. 'Call you later.' I didn't want to be free. I wanted to be Joe's love slave and I bet she was only saying that anyway because there was no one she fancied in Ireland at the moment. I remembered what Brook had said earlier about Joe falling under my spell. Maybe that's what I should do. Put a spell on him, do some magic or witchcraft. *Trouble is,* I thought, *I don't know how.* I closed my eyes and made a wish instead. *I wish I was Joe's girlfriend. I wish I was Joe's girlfriend. I wish I was Joe's girlfriend.*

11

Hocus pocus, eeny meeny miney mo and catch a falling star. Amen.

He reappeared minutes later holding a tray with two chocolate milkshakes and a huge double-choc chip cookie.

'Death by chocolate,' he said as he sat down next to me.

'Only way to go.'

'Who were you talking to?' he asked.

'Oh no one. You?'

'Mia,' he replied. 'I'd borrowed a pile of her art books and she needs them back. Sometimes the signal in here is weak. Yours worked, did it?'

I nodded.

'I'm surprised. Mine never does in here – that's why I went outside. Different networks, I guess.'

Hmm. He appeared to be on the level. No mention of getting back together with Mia. Just art books.

'So. Ruspoli,' Joe said, after we had drunk some of our milkshakes. 'Down to business. I've been thinking. I have a proposition for you.'

'Oh. OK, shoot,' I said. Last year we'd worked on the same team painting scenery for the school show. Maybe he wanted me to do something like that again.

'Me. You. How about it?' he asked and looked right into my eyes in an intense way that made my toes curl. I got the feeling it was my turn to say something, but my brain was trying to take in what he had said and work out if there was a catch.

'Me. You. How about what?'

He pointed at himself then at me. 'Couple. Us. Let's go for it. I've been thinking. New year, new chapter – all that bollards,' he said, then slid down on to one knee. 'Oh Ruspoli,' he said in a silly high voice. 'I cannot resist your seductive charms any longer. I give in. I am yours to do with what you like.'

I glanced over my shoulder. Nicky and Ruby were staring, taking it all in. Part of me was delighted that they'd seen, they are such gossips. This would definitely get around school. I turned back to Joe.

'Serious?' I asked.

He got back up on to the couch. 'Serious. No more messing.'

Heckity hoola, I thought as I drained my glass. Heaven. Joe. Chocolate. It didn't get any better.

'So?' he asked.

Be cool, be cool, I told myself. 'I may need time to consider —'

He leaned forward and kissed me again. Mush. Chocolate mush. My brain was chocolate mush.

'OK,' I said or, rather, I tried to say. It came out as a squeak. But yay, New Year's resolution number one. Sorted. Maybe Brook was right. Maybe I am witchee woman.

Chapter 3

All Change?

I could hear voices coming from the kitchen when I got home from seeing Joe. I crossed the hall and listened at the door.

'Of course he must come,' I heard Mum say. 'Sarah, this is your home, not ours. We always knew that it was a temporary arrangement.'

'But where will you go? No, Fleur, family comes first.' Aunt Sarah's voice.

I didn't mean to stay and eavesdrop; I'd intended to race upstairs to tell my news about Joe to Leela, Zahrah and Brook (I'd already told Erin as soon as I'd left Joe outside the café) but Aunt Sarah's words made me freeze. 'Where will you go?' she'd asked. Go? You? Where? I had to find out what she and Mum were talking about. *Please God, don't let whatever it is mean that we have to move again,* I prayed. That would be just my luck. Joe wants to go out with me and Mum and Dad make plans to move to the other side of the planet again.

'You've been more than generous and patient,' said Mum. 'It can't have been easy having the four of us invade your space, plus Ethan, Jess and the twins and Lewis at weekends.'

'I've loved having you,' said Aunt Sarah. 'This house is meant for a family. It was far too big for Kate and me and as you know, even though she's only in the Sixth Form, she's rarely home these days.'

'Exactly,' said Mum. 'Meant for a family and so it will be when Tom and his boys move in with you.'

Ah, I thought, *that's what it's about. Tom. Aunt Sarah's new boyfriend.* She'd been seeing him since the autumn and had kept quiet about it at first. Said she didn't want to jinx things by introducing him too soon, but he seems to have lasted the course. We met him briefly at Christmas and again for a longer time at New Year. He was OK, clearly taken with Aunt Sarah. His wife died five years ago leaving him with two boys, aged ten and eight. We haven't met them yet. They live in Wimbledon, I think. It had been nice to see Aunt Sarah happy with someone. She hadn't dated much since she split up with Kate's dad, which had always seemed a waste to me because Aunt Sarah's so stylish and attractive. *But why would Tom and the boys move in here?* I wondered.

I pushed the door open and Mum and Aunt Sarah jumped, like they'd been caught doing something they shouldn't.

'What are you talking about?' I asked.

'Oh nothing,' said Mum.

For sisters, they look completely different. Mum takes after Grandma and is a tall English rose with light auburn hair, whereas Sarah takes after Grandpa and is smaller and curvier with dark hair. Their style is different too. Mum's boho hippie in velvets and jeans, whereas Aunt Sarah wears well-cut linen or wrap dresses with expensive jewellery.

'I heard you. You were talking about moving.'

Mum got up from the chair by the Aga, came over and gave me a hug. 'Hey, don't worry, hon.'

'Don't worry? Don't *worry*? Dylan and I have only just got settled at school. I've only just made friends. Do you know how difficult that is when you're the new girl in any year after Year Seven? And, and . . .' I wasn't going to say, And I've just been asked to go steady with the one person I've fancied since last summer who happens to be one of the most sought-after boys at our school, because I felt tears come to my eyes. A wave of anxiety flooded over me and, even though I knew I'd sounded whiney, I couldn't help it.

'Hey, India Jane,' said Aunt Sarah. 'No one's going anywhere. I've been telling your mum.'

'So why were you talking about Tom moving in here?'

'Ah. So you heard,' said Aunt Sarah. 'Early days. The lease is up on the house he is renting and we have talked about him moving but, even if he does come, I won't be throwing you out. You don't need to worry. We can all live here. It's a big house. If it happens, and it's still an enormous *if* at the moment, Tom can be in with me and the boys can share the spare room. There's loads of space for all of us.'

'But this is Sarah's home, India Jane,' said Mum quietly. 'We never meant to stay for ever.'

I had to get out. I felt like I was going to say something awful or cry if I stayed. I wasn't quite sure why I was being so emotional. I'm not normally. Maybe because, even though it was Aunt Sarah's place, it did feel like home. I liked living there a lot.

Aunt Sarah picked up on my thoughts. 'It's your home too, India Jane. You have no need to worry. I'm not throwing anyone out on the street.'

I pushed past Mum to get out as Dylan came in. 'What's to eat?' he asked, then looked around. 'What's going on? Who died?'

'You will,' I said, 'if you don't get out of my way.'

'And have a nice day to you, too,' he said. 'What's your problem? Got your period?'

Twelve-year-old boys can be very irritating at times, especially know-it-all ones like my cherub-looking brother.

'No, I have not got my period,' I said.

'Then chill out. Oh and Tyler called when you were out. I

said you'd gone to meet Joe.'

'You *what*?' No! 'Why did you tell him that? And what's more, how did you even know where I'd gone?'

Dylan tapped his nose.

'If you've been reading my diary or my emails again, I *will* kill you,' I said.

Dylan looked over at Mum and shrugged. 'Do you see now what I have to put up with? Psycho sister.'

Argh, argh, argh, I thought as I went out into the hall to find my mobile in my rucksack. Tyler was a lovely boy I had met last year. He came to my rescue after I'd been mugged, then we'd been on a few dates. I liked him. I did. Just not as much as Joe. I had thought about seeing more of him, but I knew that I'd have to tell him that Joe and I were going to be an item now. I would have done anyway but wanted to do it in my own time and I'd much rather that it came from me, not my nosey-parker brother. I found Tyler's number on my phone and called. His voicemail picked up.

'Oh, um, hi Tyler, India Jane here. Returning your call. Er. Maybe see you around?' I hoped that was casual enough, friendly but not encouraging. I didn't want to tell him about dating Joe on his voicemail, but I promised myself that I would if he called back.

Duty done, I took the stairs two at a time up to my room where Posh and Becks, my black and white kittens, were sleeping on the end of my bed. The sight of them made the tears that had been threatening earlier spill out down my cheeks and I let out a loud sob. The idea that they might be homeless or that I might have to leave them was too much. I lay on my bed and had a good cry, causing Posh to raise one sleepy eye and look at me with concern.

'Don't you worry, Posh, I'll look after you,' I said. 'I won't let Mum and Dad drag you to different countries the way they have me, making me leave my friends over and over.'

Becks meowed as if he was agreeing.

After I was all cried out for the time being, I went to the bathroom. My period had arrived. Dylan, the little nuisance, had been right. And it was true, I did sometimes feel ratty when it was coming up to the time of the month and I would cry at the drop of a hat. *Even so,* I thought, *it's very annoying to be reminded of it by a small boy.*

Chapter 4

Art

As the first weeks of January went by, there was no more mention of moving out or Tom and his boys moving in. Most of my time was taken up with schoolwork and urg, yuk, argh, we had exams and assessments. I did my best – studied every night, lunchtime, breaktime, but, because I'd only joined the school last September and the syllabus was different to my previous school, I knew that I was behind my classmates. Ten subjects and each with a ton of homework. Mrs Goldman, our head of year, had been very supportive last term but, halfway through January, she called me into her office where she was sitting behind her desk looking, to my mind, like a big blond friendly rabbit. I see people as creatures sometimes and it's probably Mrs Goldman's long face and slightly large teeth that give her the bunny look. One day I will do a series of paintings of people as the animals I see in them.

'I know it's been a readjustment for you, India,' she said, as I sat in the chair that she indicated opposite her, 'but this is your second term here now and you need to buck up your ideas if you're going to stand any chance of decent results.'

'I'm doing my best, Mrs Goldman,' I said.

'I think you need to do more than that if you don't want to end up repeating your exams or even the year.'

I really didn't want to do that but it was true — I was struggling. I had opted to do ten subjects: art, English language, English literature, maths, science, French, RE, media, history and music. Sometimes it felt like I was *always* studying and, lately, I also felt a sense of panic, like there wasn't enough time to give each subject the attention it needed.

'I'll study harder,' I said but, as I said the words, I felt a knot in my stomach. More studying meant more time away from Joe. Since we'd agreed to go out, apart from hanging out at each other's houses a few times, we'd only had two proper dates, one to a movie and another for a walk in Holland Park, where we almost froze to death. Both times, I'd felt guilty, like I was skiving when I should have been home working and I didn't want to feel like that around him. Having waited a whole term to be his girlfriend, I wanted to luxuriate in every moment and hang out with him as often as possible.

Mrs Goldman looked at me with concern. 'Sometimes you have to come at your subjects another way otherwise you can get stressed. If you can incorporate some of your study into time off, it won't seem like work.'

I couldn't imagine how I could do that and my blank expression must have betrayed my feelings.

'Is there anyone you can study with, India Jane?'

I nodded. 'Maybe.' Not Brook. I'd tried with her and we ended up swapping make-up tips. Same with Leela although, instead of make-up, we'd listened to music. Zahrah wasn't really into studying with anyone else. She said it distracted her.

'Your best subjects are art and English. How about a theatre visit to see a play on the syllabus or an art gallery trip to see the work of some of the artists that you're studying? That's the sort of thing I meant,' Mrs Goldman continued. 'So you're working but not.'

I felt a light ping on in my head. Joe. He was doing art A-level. I'd never thought of him as a study partner, but he'd be brilliant. I grinned at Mrs Goldman. 'Yes. Of course. I know exactly who I can study with. Excellent,' I said. 'Thank you so much.'

'You're welcome,' she said.

I linked arms with Joe as we made our way down the South Bank the following Saturday. I'd emailed him as soon as I had got home on the evening after my session with Mrs Goldman and he seemed to like the idea of exploring London for his projects as well as mine. After that, I had spent a pleasurable hour on the computer working out an itinerary for us for the next few weekends. Bliss.

'We can see Picasso at Tate Modern,' I said, as we passed a man dressed in medieval clothes and sprayed gold who had a small crowd around him. 'But we can do all the other floors there too, if you like.'

Joe didn't appear to be listening. He pulled us to a stop to watch the gold man who was sitting on a box. 'I've seen this guy before. He's amazing. Watch. He never blinks. I've stood and watched him for ages and never caught him out, it's like he's zoned out somewhere.'

'I wonder how long it takes him to spray on that colour every morning,' I whispered back.

Joe chuckled. 'Yeah. Weird, isn't it? Like, most people getting ready for work put on a suit or something. This guy gets out the spray can.'

We stood and watched for a while and the man was completely motionless – not a blink, even when tourists tried to distract him by snapping their fingers in front of his face or sneezing loudly. I was drawn into the stillness of the moment and light-headed with happiness, like I was floating on the fluffiest cloud in the sky. It was so good to be there with Joe sharing the whole experience – the crisp, cold but sunny day, the River Thames with the boats running along to our left, the sensation of Joe's body next to mine, warm, his arm linked with

23

mine, me being his girlfriend. We were a couple, Joe and India Jane, an item, going out and this was just the beginning.

'Living art,' said Joe, as we set off again a few minutes later. As we strolled along, we passed a few different mime artists – a man dressed as a pearly king, who was having his photo taken with a Japanese tourist, a witch girl with a green face, a spaceman in high silver boots, but none of them were as good as Gold Man.

At Tate Modern, we cruised a photography exhibition together on the second floor, then we went off to look at galleries that were related to our individual studies. I was totally blown away by the work on display – bursts of colour and energy which sparked off loads of ideas of my own. After an hour, we met up on the balcony overlooking the river. There was a fabulous view of London and the river spread out in front of us. Joe took some photos, then we got a table, shared an enormous cheese and tomato baguette which we washed down with Diet Coke. I felt so grown-up and for once the panic about study had subsided.

'We had career advisers last week,' I told him when we'd finished the last crumb. 'I haven't a clue what I want to do, not really. Something to do with art I think, but what I don't know.'

'Me neither,' said Joe. 'I don't reckon you have to decide yet.'

'I do, sort of – we have to decide what subjects to take next year, for Sixth Form.'

'Choose art then. You can always change. Nothing is set in concrete.'

'I guess. And actually, I'm not sure yet but we might have to move from my Aunt Sarah's house.'

'Where to?'

'Knowing Dad, it might be anywhere. Thailand. Peru. The Outer Hebrides. You've met him so know what he's like. So restless.'

'He's great and it would be fantastic if he picks somewhere you haven't been yet. Cool. I reckon that seeing as much of the planet as possible is what life is all about.'

Joe's reaction was not what I had been hoping for, although probably to be expected as Joe got on well with Dad – like they were old pals, in fact. But I wanted Joe to ask, What about us? To say that Dad couldn't take me too far away because he'd miss me, but he didn't seem phased by the news at all. I wanted to see that he cared in the same way that Leela, Brook and Zahrah had when I had told them that I might be moving again. They were so upset. Brook said I could stay with her and share her room, Leela said she'd read up on how to do a 'stay put' spell to cast on Dad and Zahrah had given me a big hug. But Joe was so laid-back. You might move away? Whatever. He rarely showed his emotions. Suddenly a thought occurred to me. Joe was doing his A-level exams this year. I knew that he had applied for places at London universities, but loads of people these days took gap years. In fact, Joe had talked about the possibility of going abroad a few times, but I'd never thought about it actually happening. Maybe he had been serious, maybe *he'd* be leaving London!

'Er . . . What about you?' I asked trying to make my voice sound as casual as possible. 'Um. I know that you have applied to some universities but I remember you also talking about travelling. Er . . . have you decided yet?'

Joe shrugged. 'Nothing's definite, but I think I do want to take a gap year. Me and my mate Sam have talked about it. Maybe do those places you mentioned. Thailand, maybe Peru, maybe see you in one of those places if you go. I'd like to see the world before getting stuck into doing a degree or whatever. Maybe climb Machu Picchu. Maybe spend a few weeks back in Greece to earn some dosh. We'll need a fair bit to travel with, even though Mum and Dad said that they might chip in.'

The soft cloud I had been floating around on all day suddenly turned black and heavy with rain. *Noooooooooooooo,* I heard a voice inside myself groan. *Nothing is for ever. Nothing good ever lasts.*

Joe put a finger under my chin and tilted my face up to look at him. 'Hey, you OK? You've gone very quiet.'

I didn't want him to see that I was freaked out by his plan to travel. What would he think? Maybe that it was presumptuous for me to be thinking that we would even still be together in six months' or a year's time? We'd agreed to be a couple for now, not for ever. The fact that I saw us as long-term might scare a commitment-phobe like Joe right off. I made myself smile. 'I was just thinking what a great afternoon this has been. And now, this moment. I love the view of the river from up here –

London at its best. I was being all Zen and thinking, I have to be in the here and now, appreciate the present – not worry about the future and what I am going to do.' *Or what you're going to do,* I thought.

Joe looked deeply into my eyes, then he leaned over and kissed my forehead. 'Zen, huh? That's what I like about you, Ruspoli. I never know what's going on in that head of yours. Some girls are so predictable, but not you. I never know what you're going to come out with next.'

'Just call me Miss Enigma,' I said and half closed my eyes in an attempt to make myself look mysterious. If he only knew what was really going on in my head. Me, Zen. Hah! I was as far from being calm and Zen as was possible and what was really going on in my head was a voice saying, *Don't leave, Joe. Please don't leave.*

Chapter 5

Family Lunch

'So do you think Adam and Matt will move in?' asked Dylan as we fetched Mum's tiramisu dessert from the kitchen. We were having Sunday lunch on the first weekend in February and it was being served in the proper dining room at the back of the house. We had to set the table in there, because you could seat up to twenty and there wasn't enough room for all of us around the kitchen table where we normally ate. This time we were fourteen. Aunt Sarah and Kate. Mum, Dad, Ethan, his wife Jess and the twins, Eleanor and Lara. Lewis. Dylan and me and then Tom and his boys, Matt and Adam. It would have been fifteen if Joe had come – he often stayed for meals, slotting in like one of the family. That day, however, he had to go with his mum to

28

help her with her monthly shop for groceries and then he was going to play football.

'I'm beginning to think that it's a distinct possibility,' I said. 'Does it worry you?'

Dylan stopped for a moment. 'Not sure,' he said. 'What do you think of them?'

'Sweet. Shy. I think it must be hard for them.' When Tom had brought his boys into the front room to meet everyone, they'd looked terrified and younger than their respective ten and eight years. Everyone did what they could to make them feel at home and they had relaxed a little, but both of them spent a lot of time looking at the floor, stayed near their dad and were polite in the way that Dylan and I are when we are with complete strangers. Tom must have primed them beforehand to be on their best behaviour and say please and thank you. The eldest one, Adam, looked just like him, same brown hair and open face; the younger one was paler and smaller in frame with wide blue eyes. *He must take after their mum,* I thought. I felt for them. It must have been so hard losing her, making huge adjustments, and today having to come into an unfamiliar house and not just meet Kate but the whole lot of us in one go. If I had been asked, I would have told Aunt Sarah to introduce us one or two at a time, not throw them in the deep end. Meeting so many new people must have been overwhelming, but maybe she was nervous too – about bringing them into her home and wondering if they would accept her – and so wanted her family around for support. It couldn't have been easy for her either.

'Think we'll be chucked out?' asked Dylan.

'Aunt Sarah said she'd never do that.'

'Hmm. Can't see it working though, can you? I mean Aunt Sarah was single when we first came to live here. It will be different if Tom moves in. There are too many of us Ruspolis here. He'll feel outnumbered. Not at first but he will in the end. A man needs to feel his home is his castle. He won't know who is boss. Aunt Sarah? Dad? No. It could get *very* complicated. I think we have to go.' He sighed then as if he was carrying the weight of the world on his shoulders, picked up the tiramisu and took it into the dining room.

I followed him in with a dish of raspberries and strawberries. Dylan did make me smile. Some days he was a forty-year-old man trapped in a twelve-year-old body.

After Tom and the boys had gone and the rest of us were still sitting around the table chatting, Mum and Dad beckoned to Dylan, Lewis and me to follow them into the kitchen. On the way out, I noticed Dad pick up a file from the top of the sideboard.

'What is it, Dad?' asked Dylan, when we had reached the kitchen and Dad had shut the door behind us.

'I wanted to have a quiet word with you about our future —' he started.

'I knew it,' said Dylan. 'We're homeless again.'

'Why do you say that?' said Mum. 'India Jane, have you been putting ideas into his head?'

'Hey, don't blame me. He has his own ideas.'

'We won't be homeless,' said Dad. 'Of that I can assure you.'

'So what's going on then?' asked Dylan. 'Give it to us straight.' Dear Dylan, anyone would have thought he was asking if he was going to live or die after major surgery.

'OK,' said Dad. 'First sit down at the table, relax.'

We sat. We didn't relax.

'Today we met Tom and his boys,' Dad continued. 'Last week, Sarah told your mother and I that they have decided to give it a go and live together so, yes, they will be moving in. As you all know, your Aunt Sarah has been more than generous with her home these last months, but it was always meant to be a temporary arrangement while your mum and I found our feet and you two got settled at schools. Now it's time to move on.'

I felt my heart sink. *Oh Lord, here it comes. Where's it to be? India? South America? The Isle of Bongo-wunga-land?*

'Where will you go, Mum? And when?' Lewis asked. He looked as anxious as I was – even though he no longer lived with us, I knew he loved having us nearby.

'Absolutely no rush,' she replied. 'We will only go when we have found somewhere.'

'Yes, but *where*, Mum?' I asked.

Dad opened his file and put a pile of brochures on the table. 'From estate agents,' he said. 'We're on the hunt and I want you to help. It has to be somewhere reasonably near your school but probably not Holland Park. I don't think we can afford the prices here.'

'Near school? Dad, did you say near school?' I asked.

Dad nodded.

'So you won't be moving as in to another continent or country?' asked Lewis.

'Heavens no. Not the time for it. I have work with the orchestra. Your mother has work making her bath products to sell in Sarah's shop. And we need to be reasonably near if only to do your laundry, Lewis, and I want to be near my grandchildren.'

'Cheek,' said Lewis, although he couldn't deny it. He was always turning up with bin bags full of dirty washing to be done.

I could have fainted with joy. I didn't have to leave my mates or Joe. Phew, phew and phew.

'We wanted to let you know our plans first, then we will tell Ethan and the others. Kate knows about Tom moving in, but she doesn't know about us going. OK so far?' asked Dad.

Dylan shrugged. Lewis and I nodded.

'We thought now would be a good time to let everyone know while the family is gathered,' said Dad. He didn't have to wait long, because the door pushed open and all the others piled through.

'What's going on?' asked Kate.

Dylan pointed at the brochures.

'Is someone moving?' asked Ethan.

Kate flicked back her long dark hair from her face in a gesture of annoyance. 'I want my own flat,' she said.

The noise level escalated as everyone started talking at once.

'*ATTENZIONE!*' Dad called. 'You can talk later, just let me speak will you?'

Everyone shut up and turned back to him.

'Right. That's better. Now, Sarah, do you want to speak?'

'No, you go ahead,' she said.

He turned and picked up a wad of papers and brochures. 'Dylan, India Jane, Fleur and I will be moving,' he said. 'Not far. Not out of London.'

Mum got up to join him. 'I'd also like to say something. First, thanks to my lovely sister for making us feel that this was our home and I wish you all the best for your future with Tom. You deserve to be loved and you deserve to be happy.'

Sarah smiled, but I noticed Kate roll her eyes when Mum said this. I hadn't spoken to her lately and wondered how she felt about having her home invaded again. She'd been good about us moving in, considering how different it must have been to when it was just her and her mother. *Change. It upsets everything,* I thought. Sometimes I wished things could just stay as they were.

'Thank you,' said Aunt Sarah. 'Early days but . . . yes, I do feel ready, but I want to assure you all that there is no rush. Only go

33

when you have found somewhere you are happy with.'

'In that case, we're here for ever then,' said Dylan. Everyone laughed and Dylan began to polish off a bowl of crisps that were on the table as though his declaration resolved everything and we were staying put.

Afterwards, I went straight upstairs to email the girls, including Erin, and then I called Joe. I wanted to share the good news about us staying nearby, even if he hadn't seemed that bothered when I had first told him about the possible move. He sounded delighted.

'Let's celebrate. Come out,' he said. 'I'm down near Notting Hill tube, going to meet some mates later. Come and join us.'

'Cool,' I said. 'And I can help Dad and look in some estate agents' windows while I'm there.'

Half an hour later, I saw Joe sitting on a bench. He waved when he saw me, wrapped me in a big hug when I got to him and wouldn't let me go until he had almost squeezed the breath out of me.

'Excellent news,' he said, when he finally released me. 'I am so pleased you're not going away.'

'Really? Because the other day you acted like it was no big deal.'

Joe shrugged, then smiled. 'I don't always know what I'm feeling until later. Like that day you told me about the possibility of you going, it was only when I got home that I thought, Whoa, India leaving? No, that wouldn't be so great. I really like being with you and your family. I was sorry I missed the lunch today.'

'So why didn't you tell me you didn't want us to go?'

'Hey, I don't do the cling-on thing.'

I put my arms around his neck. 'I wouldn't mind. I like knowing that you care.'

'OK, in that case, I would have found you somehow. I decided that I wouldn't let a bit of distance stand in the way.'

And there was my answer as to how to deal with it if he did go travelling or away to university. I would find him too.

Five minutes later, we were joined by his mates, Sam and Chris, who were both dressed in their football kit. Both were cute but in different ways: Sam was classic tall, dark and handsome and he knew it. He even had a dimple on his chin. Chris was medium height with blue eyes and an open, friendly face.

Chris smiled and said hi – he was always friendly. Sam didn't look pleased to see me at all. No change there. He had been distant with me ever since I had started going out with Joe.

I was determined to win him over. 'And hi to you too, Sam,' I said.

Sam shrugged and without even giving me a glance said, 'I thought we were playing footie, Joe.'

'No can do,' said Joe. 'Me and India here have some celebrating to do.'

Sam now turned to me. 'But our team will be one short,' he said accusingly. 'And you brought your football gear with you, didn't you?'

Joe nodded and indicated his sports bag on the ground next to him.

I got up. 'Hey, I would never stand between a man and his football,' I said. 'You go, Joe. I've got a lot to do.'

'No, er . . . I know,' he said. 'Come with us. I won't play for long, then we can go and do something.'

Sam's expression darkened.

'Actually, Joe, I am way behind on work,' I said. 'I really ought to go back and study. You go.'

'Sure?' asked Joe.

'Yeah, she's sure,' droned Sam.

'OK, then I'm just going to get some water,' said Joe. 'Don't go yet, India Jane.'

'I'll come with you,' said Chris and the two of them disappeared into a nearby mini supermarket.

'Make the most of it,' said Sam, when they were out of earshot. 'You do know that Joe's record for dating a girl is three months.'

'So I have some time to go,' I said. I wasn't going to let him intimidate me. 'And I like a challenge. Maybe I can break the record.'

'They all think that,' he replied. He gave me such a cold look, and I thought, *What have I ever done to you?* but I was determined not to let him see that he made me nervous.

'So nice to meet you properly, Sam,' I said.

He didn't reply. With a shrug, he turned away and looked in the window of the supermarket.

On my way home after the boys had gone, I called Leela and filled her in.

'Jealous,' she said. 'Boys get very precious about their buddy-buddy time.'

'Maybe.'

'Definitely.'

'It made me think too. I've never had a proper boyfriend before as in "going steady" and it has made me realise something. He comes with a package. Friends. Mates.'

'And family,' said Leela. 'Sometimes pets too. Don't forget them. Never get between a man and his dawg.'

I laughed and, after we'd finished our call, I went to look in estate agents' windows. It had never occurred to me to ask or care if Joe liked my mates, nor if they liked him although they seemed to. When I thought about it, it was definitely love me, love my mates. They were a huge part of my life. I suppose that went for his friends too, although I could never imagine getting on with Sam. *Just because I like Joe doesn't mean that I will automatically like his choice of mates. Maybe I should organise a get-together with us all. Zahrah would soon sort moody Sam out,* I thought as I looked at the prices of houses and flats and

37

immediately saw why Dad had said we couldn't afford to stay in the area. You needed megabucks to buy even a one-bed flat in Holland Park.

Later that evening, I was upstairs studying when my phone beeped that I had a text. It was from Joe.

Look out of your window.

I did as I was told and saw that Joe was on the opposite side of the street. He waved when he saw me and beckoned that I should go down. A quick slick of lip-gloss and I grabbed my jacket and keys, then took the stairs down two at a time. All was quiet on the ground floor apart from the sound of the television in the living room. I snuck past, opened the door quietly and went out to join Joe.

'Hey,' he said. 'Did I disturb your studying?'

'No rest for the wicked.'

Joe grinned and there was a twinkle in his eye. 'Wicked? We haven't even started yet.'

'Is that right?'

'Yeah. I felt bad deserting you before.'

'No problem,' I said.

'I just wanted to say good night.'

'Good night? It's only seven o'clock.'

'So can you come out for a bit?'

I laughed. 'A bit of what?'

He pulled me towards him, put my arms around his neck and

kissed me. I didn't care who saw. I didn't even care if Mum and Dad had heard me go and were looking out of the front window. Joe tasted of mints, his arms felt warm and his lips were soft. *I am in love,* I thought. *And this is so much more fun than homework.*

Chapter 6

Head or Heart?

'How was school, India Jane?' asked Mum.

I rolled my eyes. 'Major stressful. Decisions, decisions, decisions. What I want to do when I leave. What I want to do in the Sixth Form. It's doing my head in. Should I do art or something more academic? I don't know.'

It was suppertime on Wednesday evening and we had all just tucked into bowls of linguini made by Dad. No one was in a great hurry to leave the table, which is usual with our family, plus it was so cold outside, threatening snow, it felt nice to be inside huddled together cosy and warm. I don't think I could have got up anyway, because Dad is a fab cook and my stomach was about to burst.

'It's all very well being artistic,' said Aunt Sarah, 'but with the creative arts – dance, music, painting and drama – there's so much competition at university and beyond.'

'But she must follow her heart,' said Dad. 'She has a natural talent for drawing.'

'And sadly, so do hundreds of others,' said Aunt Sarah. 'I have friends who see people's portfolios every week, designers looking for work and, believe me, there is some astounding talent out there. And I've seen your new project, India Jane, the portraits of your friends – they are very good. But it's not enough to be creative. You have to work out how to use your creativity so you can make a living.'

I had got started on my art project back in January and I was pleased with what I had done so far. I'd taken photos of the girls' profiles then done a series of drawings and, next, I was going to do paintings in different colours to show their different personalities. Shades of pink for Leela, cool pastels for Brook and maybe no nonsense black and white for Zahrah. I had also asked Erin to send a recent photo so that I could include her. Her paintings would be green of course, because of her Irish roots.

'I reckon you should do something practical,' said Dylan. 'Something that people will always need – like a plumber or a nurse or a hairdresser. People will always need haircuts.'

'Yeah right. I'll cut yours later if you like,' I offered with a smile.

'On second thoughts, forget that,' said Dylan. 'I remember

you tried to cut my hair before and it was all lopsided.'

'I was trying to start a fashion.'

Dad got up and began to clear the table and Dylan got up to join him.

'The thing that's important is not to identify too closely with a job or career,' said Dad. 'I think that is wrong. You have to find your true self beyond how you choose to make money to live. That is not who you are. So many people after a certain age believe that their job is who they are – a teacher, a shopkeeper, a builder. That is not who they are, that is what they do. Who you are is your core, that spirit, the soul that lives inside of you.'

Kate crossed her eyes and made a peace sign.

Mum nodded in agreement with Dad but Aunt Sarah sighed. 'Finding who you are is all very well, but it doesn't always pay the bills or the mortgage. It's India Jane's time of life when she has to make some career choices. Choose some subjects to study in the Sixth Form. Think forward about how she's going to get ahead in life, what she wants. And anyway, who says you can't still find yourself if you have a career? My path hasn't exactly been conventional but, India, I think you need to look realistically at how you can aim for the right career where, OK, you can be your true self, but can also have some security.'

I nodded. 'Exactly.'

It was so typical for Dad to go off on one of his rants about being true to yourself and following your heart and it wasn't that I didn't think there was anything in what he said, it was just

I couldn't imagine it would go down well in class when we were discussing career choices. 'Yes, Mrs Goldman, I am going to follow my heart, be myself and let the Force be with me, that's what I am going to do.' I'd be laughed out of the classroom. Sometimes Dad lived in his own idealistic bubble, out of touch with mainstream life, but then he was a lot happier than a lot of men his age who I saw hurrying to work in suits in the morning and looking grumpy. Dad had refused to be tied down to one job and he could turn his hand to anything, whether it was making delicious meals, playing the piano, writing poetry, making furniture – he could even knit. Mum said he was a Renaissance man, which apparently is a romantic way of saying that someone is an all-rounder. *On the other hand,* I thought as I watched him clear away the dishes, *although he has had a colourful life and we have lived in countries that some people only dream about, we haven't got a home and Mum and Dad haven't got any savings. Small set-back.*

Before supper, we'd looked at various estate agents' lists and it wasn't looking hopeful, although Dylan was still occupied sifting through them all, determined to find something that had been missed. I knew it was futile as I'd discovered when I had looked in estate agents' windows: no way could Mum and Dad afford the prices of houses, not in Holland Park nor in areas nearby. Of course Aunt Sarah had emphasised that we could stay as long as needed, but Dad told her that instead of buying a house, he was going to look into renting as an option.

'Hey, you could always be a drug dealer,' said Kate. 'We're in a good area for it and, as Dylan said, best to do something for which there is always a demand. Notting Hill Gate has always been a druggie area.'

I glanced over at Aunt Sarah. She looked cross. 'I suppose you think that's amusing, do you, Kate?' she asked. 'Why do you always have to try and shock people? It's not clever and it's not funny and we all know you don't mean it.'

Kate got up and sloped to the door. I always marvelled at how slim she was, even though she ate twice as much as the rest of us sometimes, she always stayed slinky skinny-model gorgeous. 'Why don't you all leave her alone? It's India Jane's life. She's the one who has to decide,' she said, then turned to me. 'I still don't know what I want to do. Don't let it bug you. And don't let any of them talk you into anything you don't want to do. It's your life.'

I noticed that Aunt Sarah was chewing her bottom lip, clearly trying to bite back something she wanted to say. She and Kate often clashed, and it was true that Kate often went out of her way to say whatever was opposite to what everyone else was saying just to get a reaction.

'Times have changed,' said Mum, after Kate had left the room and Dad had brought a bowl of pears and a plate of cheese to the table. 'Once people could choose a career path and pursue it all their life.'

'Or be stuck with it all their life,' said Dad.

'These days, it's different,' Mum continued. 'Times keep changing and people sometimes find themselves made redundant so they have to adapt, change jobs. In fact, many people have a few careers before they retire.'

'It's true. India, love,' said Aunt Sarah. 'Don't listen to Kate. We're not trying to tell you what to do here. It's a discussion and, although I suppose Kate is entitled to her opinion, your mother's right. The more strings to your bow, the greater your chance of survival. My advice would be that there's no harm in picking a couple of avenues to pursue.'

'So are you saying that the choice is to follow your heart, your dream, and risk not having security *or* find a good steady career and know that there is regular money coming in?' I asked.

'Not exactly. It's not always that clear cut. I am saying, try to have some idea of where you want to go and pick your subjects with that in mind,' said Aunt Sarah.

I glanced over at Mum. She wasn't saying very much and I got the feeling that was because, after years of her and Dad following their dream, they had very little to show for it, whereas Aunt Sarah had always ploughed away, stayed in one place and worked hard to make a base for her and Kate. Now she had loads of dosh and a fab house but then, for all her wealth, there had been days before Tom came along when she looked sad – she had no husband, she had an uneasy relationship with her daughter and had been lonely before we landed on her doorstep. At least Mum and Dad had each other and were happy. God, it was complicated. I was beginning to feel seriously depressed. Jobs. Careers. Goals. It was all anyone talked about these days at school and at home and everyone had an opinion but me. I still hadn't a clue which way I wanted to go apart from bed most nights, because my brain was exhausted with trying to decide and trying to keep up with doing ten subjects.

Later that same evening, Joe emailed to say hi. He often did these days if we hadn't been back to each other's house or hadn't had time together in the day. He'd either send an email or a text message or he'd go on MSN or call. I really liked the easiness of it and how he had just fitted in as part of my life. I sat down to email him back.

> *Hi Joe,*
> *Everyone here advising me what to do when I leave school. Kate suggested drug dealer. Dylan plumber or hairdresser?! Is doing my head in. What do you think I should be?*
> *Love*
> *India Jane*
> *XXX*

I deleted the love. He might think that I was saying that I loved him and it was far too early for that.

I wrote, *With best wishes.* I deleted that. Far too formal-sounding.

I wrote, *Bye for now, India Jane XXX.*

I deleted two of the XXs. Joe always did one X. He might think XXX was excessive and feel suffocated. Heckity hoola, it was mad. With a mate, I could do not only love but lots of love and endless kisses and hearts coming off the page and she wouldn't even think twice about it. What was it about boys that girls always had to be so careful how they signed off?

I sent my email and went on to MSN to see if Erin was there, as she often was in the evening.

Cinnamongirl: You there, dingbat girl?

Irishbrat4eva: Course. Doing my boring French homework and waiting *pour vous, tu,* you.

Cinnamongirl: Is doing my head in not knowing what to do when I leave school.

Irishbrat4eva: Me too. Any ideas?

Cinnamongirl: Dad says I should follow my heart.

Irishbrat4eva: Why? Is it doing a walkabout? Haha. But follow your heart and do what? Do you think we decide or life decides?

Cinnamongirl: What are you on about?

Irishbrat4eva: Fate. I have been doing *le* very deep thinking about life and stuff and wondering – fate or choice? Do we choose what to do in that we have to make things happen? Or is it all predestined? And life will guide us? What do you think my little cinnamon pal?

47

Cinnamongirl: Bejasus, Erin. It's enough I have to decide my subjects for Sixth Form without having to think about stuff like that too.

Irishbrat4eva: Oh come on, play the game. Fate or choice? Does choice or chance determine destiny?

Cinnamongirl: Both. I think you have to do as much as you can, make the choices and then fate can intervene. Maybe.

Irishbrat4eva: Good answer. Ish. You should be a diplomat.

Cinnamongirl: Yeah right. After talking to my lot downstairs, it seems to me that we have to decide between two options. Either do a job you possibly don't like so much but gives you security and you can pay the bills and mortgage and feel safe, or follow your dream but that may be risky but you might be happier but maybe it won't give financial security. So it's not between choice or chance according to my family, it's between your heart and head.

Irishbrat4eva: I think we should go for gold. Go for both options. Why not? Find something that gives us security, a cheque in the bank and all, but something that makes us happy too. It happens for some people. Some people find a job they love.

Cinnamongirl: Go for gold. Guess you have to know what you want to do first though.

Irishbrat4eva: I guess – which takes us back to square one. What do we want to do? Be happy. Guess that's what everyone wants.

My email alert pinged that I had a message. It was from Joe.

I have a suggestion for your future and that is that you be my love slave.
Joe XXX

Three kisses. Three. XXX. Yahey. Excellent. I went back to MSN.

Cinnamongirl: Joe just emailed. Said I should be his love slave.

Irishbrat4eva: Noooooooooo. That makes him your master and this is the age of equality. Email him back and say you don't accept the position because you are a liberated female. By the way, Mum said that I can get a webcam for my computer so we can do Skype and see each other!

Cinnamongirl: Fabbie. I asked Aunt Sarah already if I can use the one from her office and she said yes. When will you get it?

Irishbrat4eva: Soon. And then you will be able to see if I am picking my nose when I talk to you.

Cinnamongirl: Ergh.

But she had a point. Not about picking noses but about seeing each other. Some days when I spoke on the phone or MSN or whatever, I didn't care what I looked like because no one could see me but, with a webcam, I would have to be more careful. Especially if Joe ever got a camera! I wasn't sure he would like the bag-lady look that I favoured most weekend mornings.

After I'd finished on the computer, I sat down to do my homework. I wasn't any closer to knowing what I wanted to do in the future, so I decided to try and focus on the present and the great stacks of books and projects awaiting my attention. I could see the appeal of saying to hell with it all, I'm following my heart – it was a great excuse not to do any real work and turn on the telly instead.

My head won. I opened my books and began work.

Chapter 7

Green-eyed Monster

'Hey India Jane,' said a male voice, as I was sitting in Starbucks reading a book for history while waiting for Joe on Saturday morning. I was early for our meeting and had just been thinking about how happy I was with him and how great it was being in a couple. I turned to see a tall black boy looking down at me. It was Tyler, the boy who had rescued me the term before from muggers. He was looking as handsome as ever and I felt myself blush as I felt a tug of chemistry. It was there, no doubt about it. *But it's there with Joe too,* I told myself, *and you chose him. Behave!*

'Hi, how are you?'

'Good,' he said and he looked around. 'You on your own?'

I nodded. 'Meeting someone later.'

Why didn't you tell him it was Joe that you're meeting? asked a voice in my head.

I don't know and please shut up, said another one. I really am a typical Gemini, sign of the twins, always two voices in my head. Sometimes they have long conversations or arguments.

'Can I join you, then?' asked Tyler.

'Sure.'

We got some drinks, banana smoothie for me, hot chocolate with marshmallows for him, then we sat and caught up on the last few weeks. It felt good to spend some time with him again because, as well as the kudos of being with the best-looking boy in the café (until Joe arrived of course), I admired him. He'd told me about his future plans when I first met him and was someone who clearly got things done. He wanted to be a journalist, to make a difference and he reckoned that a good way to reach people was with words.

'Must be so nice to be sure about what you want to do,' I said after he'd told me more about his plans to study.

'Yeah, it is. Remember I told you that my uncle in New York got me some work experience on the paper he works on?'

I nodded. It was just after Tyler had helped me that he had disappeared off to the States.

'Well, that only confirmed that writing is what I want to do,' Tyler continued. 'But what about you? What do you want to do?'

'Just get through the next few months,' I replied. 'Does that make me a bad person? Because I don't know what I want to do in life. I don't have any burning ambition. I wish I did, things would be easier. I felt like I was going mad last week with everyone giving me their opinion, feeling like a light-weight around people like you and my mates, especially Zahrah. Now I've decided to be Zen about it and take it day by day.'

Tyler laughed. 'Isn't taking it day by day the Alcoholics Anonymous philosophy for life?'

I laughed with him. 'Is it? Oops. Maybe I'll be an alcoholic if I think like one already.'

Tyler reached out and took my hand. 'Nah. Not just them. It's a good philosophy; I think it's great that you think that way. I mean, we can miss so much of our lives by not being in the present, you know? Living for the future, planning our life away and missing what's really happening now.'

Handsome, clever and wise, I thought, as I gazed into his big brown eyes and wondered if he meant missing what's happening with us. *Have I been mad to let him go?*

'My Sensei said something like that too,' I said.

'Sensei?'

I nodded. It was my chance to show Tyler that I wasn't a total light-weight. I had deep thoughts too, sometimes. 'Yeah. When I was in Greece last summer, I did some meditation classes with a man called Sensei. He talked a lot about how true happiness lies in the present moment but, like you just said, most of us have got caught up in thinking happiness lies anywhere else but now – like, happiness lies on Friday when school is finished. Happiness lies when I meet the perfect boy. Happiness lies when I get that dress I saw in a shop window. He said we are missing a lot of our life by being caught up in what he called the cycle of desire.'

Tyler looked impressed and I noticed that he was still holding my hand. His eyes dropped to my mouth and I felt another rush of chemistry. I remembered kissing him. It had felt good. Really good. It was after our first date and he had kissed me not far from Aunt Sarah's house and Dylan had come out and done a number, telling us off for snogging in public.

'How's that bossy little brother of yours?' asked Tyler, who was clearly having the same kind of thoughts as I was.

I laughed. 'Dylan. Oh, still telling everyone what to do. He's twelve going on forty.'

At that moment, I became aware that someone was watching us. I glanced at the window and my heart almost stopped. There was Joe looking in at us, at my hand in Tyler's. I pulled my hand away and waved to Joe. He gave a short wave back, then headed for the door. *How long had he been there?* I wondered as I glanced at my watch.

I put on my cheeriest face when he appeared beside us a few moments later. 'Joe, this is Tyler, Tyler, Joe.'

'Ah, so this is Joe,' said Tyler. 'Your brother said that you were out with him one time when I called.'

I nodded. I remembered, I'd wanted to kill Dylan at the time.

Joe gave me a quizzical look, as if to say, Who is this boy and what's he doing calling you? Joe nodded in reply to Tyler. Not unfriendly but not friendly either. 'Yeah. I'm Joe. Have we met before? You look familiar?'

Tyler shook his head. 'Not met, but I have seen you. I came to your school show with India Jane just before Christmas. I saw you there.'

This wasn't going well. I remember that Joe had clocked Tyler and Tyler had clocked Joe after the show. 'Oh yes, Joe and I were on the scenery painting team, weren't we, Joe?' I babbled, then continued to rabbit on for the next few minutes about who was on the team and how I'd been landed the job even though I was new in school. Blabber, blabber, blabber – even the twins in my head were in agreement saying, *Shut up, India Jane*, and *Shut up now*. Why hadn't I introduced Joe as my boyfriend? What was the matter with me?

Tyler stood up. 'OK, I got to go. India J, lovely to see you. Give me a bell, hey? Maybe we can talk some more about what you want to do, but my advice would be, don't fret it. Try some different work experience if you can and see how you get on. Worked for me.'

Talk about it some more? Not if Joe can help it, I thought when I saw the expression on Joe's face at Tyler's suggestion.

'Yeah. Really good to see you.' I stood up and Tyler gave me a hug and a light kiss on the cheek.

Joe gave him an indifferent wave and sat down on the sofa. I sat next to him and Tyler disappeared out of the door and out on to the street.

'What a tosser,' Joe commented.

'Tosser? What do you mean, tosser?'

Joe rolled his eyes. 'So silky smooth. I mean, just look at the way he was dressed. All in black. Not a stitch out of place. Obviously gay.'

I burst out laughing. 'Tyler is so not gay,' I blurted.

'Oh and you know that for a fact, do you?'

'As a matter of fact —' I started then bit my lip. What was I going to say? I know because I snogged him? 'I just know he's not. OK?'

Joe wasn't going to let it go. 'How? How long have you been seeing him?'

'Not at all. We just bumped into each other that's all. He's the boy who came to my rescue when I got mugged that time. Remember? I told you.'

'Oh yeah, your knight in shining armour.'

'Kind of. He's really nice and I think that was sound advice to give things a try if I can, you know, work experience.'

'Maybe.' All of Joe's body language was closed. His arms crossed over his stomach. His legs crossed. I had never seen him like this. I squidged over so that I was closer to him and tried to link my arm through his. He immediately got up and jerked his chin towards the counter. 'Going to get something. Do you want anything or did lover boy get you something already?'

'I'm good,' I said and indicated my empty glass.

As he went off towards the counter, I felt angry. Nothing had happened with Tyler. It was totally innocent. How dare Joe act like I'd been cheating on him when I hadn't? Part of me felt like getting up and walking out.

Our first row. Maybe being in a couple wasn't so great after all.

Chapter 8

Friends

On Sunday, I woke when my alarm went off at eight o'clock. I had set it so that I could get up early and put in a full day's studying. I had made a promise to myself. All day. No distractions. No phone calls. No looking at Facebook, emails or MSN.

I woke again at nine. Oh God, I'd gone straight back to sleep.

'Why didn't you wake me?' I asked Posh who was curled up at the end of my bed. I made myself get up, staggered into the bathroom, showered, then downstairs for a cup of coffee, muffin and honey and then up to work. No putting it off. The house felt quiet as I went back up the stairs. *Everyone is having a lie in,* I thought. *Maybe I could just have another half-hour kip?*

No, I told myself. *You must work. Must. Must. Must.*

I got my books out and opened them on the pages I wanted to study. The scene the day before with Joe was still bugging me though, I kept replaying it in my mind and found it hard to concentrate. When he had come back with his drink, things hadn't improved and the atmosphere between us had felt strained. I had been cross with him and he had gone into a sulk, and after a while he'd made an excuse about having to meet up with Sam and Chris. I'd said, 'Whatever,' like I couldn't care less in order to show him that I wasn't buying into his jealous act and, when we'd parted, he kissed my cheek like I was some aged aunt. Our first row and it had felt bad. *Maybe I should have a chat with Zahrah before I start work,* I thought as I checked my watch. She was bound to be up and was the only one of my mates to have a steady boyfriend. She had been going out with a boy called Ryan for a while, so maybe she had some experience of how to deal with rows, though I had never heard her talk about having them. She and Ryan seemed blissfully in tune.

I picked up the phone and dialled her number.

'Hi, is Zahrah there?' I asked, when one of her sisters picked up.

'No, she's out.'

'Do you know when she'll be back?'

'No.'

'Do you know where she's gone?'

'Nope.'

59

I tried her mobile but it went to voicemail. *OK, work, work,* I told myself. *It's a sign I am meant to work.* Another voice suggested, *Maybe call Leela first.* I resisted for half an hour but was still finding it hard to concentrate. I needed to talk to someone. I dialled her number.

'Hi, is Leela there?'

'I think she was meeting Zahrah somewhere,' her mother told me.

Next I tried Brook. By now, it was urgent that I talk to someone about Joe. My future exam results depended on it. I got the answering machine and, when I tried her mobile, it went straight to voicemail. *Where are they all?* I wondered.

'Grrrr,' I said to Posh, who was still sleeping on the end of my bed and had now been joined by Becks. They looked so funny, both of them lying on their backs with their legs stretched out as far as they would go. I had to go and tickle their tummies. I couldn't resist.

Mum popped her head round the door. 'Morning, darling. You had breakfast?'

I nodded. She came in and sat next to me and joined in the tummy tickling and the two cats wriggled with pleasure. Mum looked over at my books. 'You're up early for a Sunday.'

I nodded. 'I've got so much to do.'

Mum put her hand on my arm. 'Is it too much, India Jane? I've been worried about you lately. I know it was a big move for you last year at this point in your schooling and on top of that we'll be moving house again soon. In fact, I think your dad and I have found a house that will do nicely. Needs a bit of work but it has the space we need. We'll take you round to see it soon.'

Tears came into my eyes and I quickly brushed them away.

'Hey, India, what is it?' asked Mum.

'Nothing. Really. I'm fine.' I felt as surprised by the tears as Mum was. 'Just, I don't know. Maybe it has all been a bit much. Like, I feel like I am just getting ahead with one subject and then another pile of work comes in for another one and I feel like I'm not giving all my subjects the proper attention. It's like that stage act, you know, when a man balances five plates on the end of five poles – only, with me, it's like I just get all the plates up and the one at the end starts to fall down, I run to that one and one at the other end falls. I can't keep them all in the air at the same time.'

'Ten subjects is a lot,' said Mum.

'It's what everyone else is doing.'

'Yes, but they have all been there since the beginning. The syllabus is still new to you.'

I indicated the books. 'Which is why I am working on a Sunday again, or rather not working. I've been faffing about like Queen of Faff.'

Mum looked at me with a concerned expression. 'We're all good at faffing when we have work to do. Don't beat yourself up. Life has to be a balance, you know. At least you have Joe to go out with and have a good time.'

It was all very well for her. She didn't have a posse of teachers snapping at her heels about her work and Mrs Goldman telling her to 'buck her ideas up'. And I wasn't sure that I did have Joe any more either. Mum didn't understand. No one did. I sighed wearily.

'Has something happened? You haven't broken up, have you?'

'Not exactly, but we might. We kind of had a row,' I said and I filled her in on what had happened the day before.

Mum listened patiently, then smiled. 'I think it's sweet that he got so jealous, don't you? Better that than he didn't care.'

'He was so sulky though, Mum. You should have seen him, like a girl pouting! And it wasn't as if anything had happened with Tyler.'

'OK. Now put yourself in his shoes. How would you have felt if you had seen him holding hands with someone? Some very pretty girl and you'd walked in on them?'

I hadn't thought of that. I imagined Joe with another girl. I didn't like it one bit. I laughed. 'Insanely jealous, I guess. I would have imagined all sorts had been going on. I would have wanted to kill him and her.'

Mum laughed. 'So there you go. He reacted because he likes you and is possessive and that's sweet really. And it's not as if he's like that all the time. He must have felt threatened.'

I felt my anger towards Joe disappear in a flash. 'I could have been more understanding, I suppose,' I said.

'It takes time sometimes,' said Mum. 'Relationships aren't always sweetness and light. Some days are going to be like that. And trying to understand where your boyfriend is coming from is part of growing up. If we all walked away at the first misunderstanding, there'd be no hope.'

I couldn't wait to see Joe again. I wouldn't be mad with him any more. I'd show him what he meant to me. I felt better after having talked to Mum and managed to get focused and down to some work.

Around three in the afternoon, Brook called. 'Hey, India Jane,' she said. 'I got your message.'

'Where've you been?' I asked. 'I've been trying to reach you and Leela and Zahrah.'

'We're in Greenwich. Sorry I didn't get back to you earlier, but we've been having the most amazing time and, we all forgot to check our messages. It's like being on holiday here. We've been around the markets and —'

As she enthused away, I couldn't help but feel jealous. They had been out without me. 'Why didn't you ask me to come?'

'Oh,' said Brook. 'Um. We assumed that you'd be doing something with Joe.'

'No. I've been at home all day, studying, it's been really boring.' I didn't say that I would have had to stay at home to catch up on work, even if they had asked me to go. 'But Zahrah has a boyfriend too. Why didn't you assume that she'd be with him?'

'Because she makes sure she never misses out on seeing us,' said Brook. 'It's different with you and Joe. You spend all your spare time with him now.'

'Do I?'

'Yes.'

I hadn't noticed. I hadn't had a lot of spare time because of trying to catch up with work so I hadn't realised that I had been neglecting my mates, but when I cast my mind back over the last few weeks, I realised that Brook was right. Outside school, I hadn't seen them once.

'God, Brook, you're right. I am sorry. Tell Leela and Zahrah too.'

'Couple bubble, just like Leela said. 'You've gone into a couple bubble.'

'Noooo. I have gone into a studying bubble. Oh God. And you've been talking about me! Will you still be my friends?'

Brook laughed. 'Hold on, I will ask the others.' The phone went quiet for a few moments then she came back on. 'Course, dingbat brain. Friends for ever.'

'Phew,' I said. 'Because no boy is worth losing friends over.'

'Exactly,' said Brook.

After she'd hung up, I sat and looked out of the window for a while. Being in a relationship really wasn't easy. First of all, learning that a boy comes with friends I might not get on with, like Sam. Second, learning to put myself in Joe's shoes. Third, learning not to neglect my mates and keep the balance. Work, love. None of it was a breeze.

'India, you have a visitor,' I heard Mum call up the stairs.

'Who is it?' I called back.

'It's me,' said Joe's voice. 'I'm coming up.'

'No, I'll come down,' I called.

Ohmigod, I thought. *I look a state.* I scrabbled to try and brush my hair and put lip-gloss on at the same time, but too late. Joe was at the door. He burst in and fell to his knees. 'Sorry, sorry, I have been such a prat.'

I laughed. 'OK, you can get up now.'

'No, no, must grovel at your feet,' he said and he grabbed my ankles and somehow wrestled me to the ground where he put his arms around me and kissed me. I hoped that Mum or Dad didn't walk in and catch us, because I didn't think they'd be too happy to find us locked on to each other on the floor. As we kissed, a song flashed through my head; I couldn't remember the exact words but they were something, like, '*The best part of breaking up is when you're making up.*' *So true,* I thought because Joe was being really passionate and so was I – our best kissing session so far. However, I mentally added another point to my list of things that were hard about being in a long-term relationship: boyfriend seeing me at my worst when I have a spot on my nose, no concealer, am in my trackie bottoms and my hair needs washing. Luckily, Joe hadn't seemed to notice.

Chapter 9

Sink or Swim

'Here we are,' said Dad, as he drew up outside a row of terraced houses in Queen's Park. 'Number seventy-two. Our new home.'

I got out of the car, glanced up at the house and my heart sank. It was horrible. There was a black wrought-iron gate falling off its hinges, a small front garden full of dead weeds and rubbish, a mouldy-looking old chair in the corner with its stuffing falling out and the doors and windows looked like they needed a good clean and lick of paint.

'Are you serious?' asked Dylan, as he and Mum joined Dad and me at the gate. 'This place is a dump.'

I burst out laughing. 'Don't hold back, Dylan.'

'I won't.' He looked well fed up.

Dad pulled keys out, went and opened the front door then ran back to the gate, gathered Mum up into his arms and carried her over the threshold like she was a new bride. Dylan rolled his eyes as a couple of Indian ladies in saris walked past, stared at them and giggled to each other.

Inside, Dad gave us what he called the 'grand tour'. It wasn't grand at all. The hallway was narrow and smelled musty; in fact, all the rooms had a damp feeling. Upstairs were four bedrooms, three on the first floor, one of which was the size of a broom cupboard with a tiny window high on the wall, too high to see out of, but the other two were spacious. The fourth room on the top floor was a good size too, with a sloping ceiling on one side. The kitchen and bathroom had modern units but, like the rest of the house, they looked like they needed a good clean.

Dylan's mood didn't improve when he saw that, like the front garden, the back was overgrown with weeds.

He came back into the hall, sat heavily on the bottom stair and he looked totally miserable. 'I think I'd like to stay with Aunt Sarah,' he said.

'Not an option,' said Dad, and he stepped up behind Dylan and sat on the stair just above him. 'We're a family and we stay together. Come on, everyone, sit. Family conference.'

Mum sat next to Dylan and put her arm around him and I went up to sit on the stair behind Dad.

'I know it's not what we've been used to,' said Dad. 'We've been very privileged to have lived in some of the most glorious locations in the world and then of course Sarah's house is wonderful, but things have changed and it's either adapt or . . . well, that's it really, no options. We have to adapt. Make the most of it. Sink or swim. We swim.'

'When life gives you lemons, make lemonade, yeah right, Dad,' said Dylan in his most gloomy voice.

'This isn't the first place we've looked at you know,' said Mum. 'While you two have been at school, we've been to see over forty houses —'

'Then a colleague of mine in the orchestra told me about this place. I know it doesn't look much now. His last tenants, students I think, left it in a right state, which is why he was so eager for it to go to people like us who will look after it. The big plus is that the rent is very low, and that will allow us to save so that in time we can buy our own place.'

'And also,' Mum joined in, 'he said we can do what we like – paint, decorate, put up pictures. Now that is something that a lot of landlords don't allow but we have a free rein here.'

Dad stood up. 'Yes. I like a challenge and, scruffy house, YOU ARE A CHALLENGE. We will make you beautiful. Stylish. People will be *amazed*. You have been neglected but no longer. The Ruspolis are here. It is your time in the limelight.'

'Er, Dad, you're talking to a house,' I said.

'And why not? It's a nice house. It has potential. It needs

some TLC that's all and we're just the people to give it. Come on, we're creative people. What do you think, India Jane?'

I shrugged a shoulder. 'Which room do you want Dylan? You can have first pick,' I said.

Dylan copied me and shrugged a shoulder, like he didn't care.

'How about Dad and I take the front room?' said Mum. 'Dylan, you have the big one at the back; the tiny one will do for when Lewis stays over, so how about the top room for you, India Jane. How does that sound?'

'Whatever,' said Dylan. He wasn't playing along at all.

'Are you happy with that arrangement, India Jane?' asked Dad.

I nodded.

'Why don't you have a think about how you might like your room decorated?' Mum asked.

'Um, I'll go and have another look,' I said. Although I felt the same way as Dylan, I didn't want to let on to Mum and Dad. I knew it was an upheaval for them too, because last night, they had left their bedroom door slightly open and I'd seen them standing with their arms around each other looking sad, and then Dad had said something about letting us down and Mum had given him a big hug. They hadn't seen me and I'd crept away before they did.

'And Dylan, let me know if you have any ideas,' said Mum.

'Burn the place down?' he replied.

I couldn't help but laugh. My sentiments exactly, but I liked what Dad had said: we could maybe do something with the house and, anyway, we had no choice. We had to make it work. *Sink or swim, win or lose, live or die and all that,* I thought, as I got up and trooped back up the stairs to think about what might be done up there.

We moved into the new house over the next few days, seeing as it was half-term. Posh and Becks were as indignant as Dylan had been at first and objected loudly when they were shut in the tiny room until we got things sorted. I was determined to make the best of it, although I had felt like crying when I saw all my stuff packed up and my lovely room at Aunt Sarah's bare. I thought about all the luxuries we had taken for granted there. State of the art showers. Top of the range TVs. Big American fridge. All the mod cons I wouldn't be able to use any more, and I hadn't even had a chance to use Aunt Sarah's webcam to talk to Erin. Dad told us all we had to be like Buddhist monks, detached from worldly goods, and he made us chant *nam myoho renge kyo* all the way in the car to the new house at the top of our voices. He said that the chant means something about dedicating oneself to the harmony and rhythm of life. How that was going to help, I couldn't imagine. He really is bonkers sometimes, but it seemed to do the trick and took my mind off feeling sad and I think it gave some people in cars near to us a laugh – four people singing their heads off is not a sight you see every day.

A couple of hours after we had arrived, Zahrah, Leela and Brook turned up each with a house-warming present: a scented candle from Brook (I had told her the place smelled musty), a chill out CD from Zahrah that she had put together herself and some scrummy yummy Indian sweets from Leela that her aunt had made specially. We got my CD player out, put the CD on, lit the candle and ate the sweets, no problemo.

'Home,' I said gloomily, as I looked around at the mess and the unpacked bags and the wallpaper peeling off the wall to my right. The others followed my gaze, then Leela lay back and started laughing. 'Home,' she repeated in a deep, sad voice.

'My smelly bedroom,' said Brook in an even gloomier voice.

'I'd love my own bedroom,' said Zahrah. 'At least you don't have to share.'

'She does,' said Leela. 'With all the dust mites and bedbugs.'

We all cracked up laughing.

Zahrah went over to look out of the window. 'Hey, you've got a nice view from here.'

I got up from the bed to join her. The window looked out over the cricket grounds and then over towards Notting Hill Gate.

'How will you get to school?' asked Leela.

'Bus,' I said. 'The stop is near, so that's no sweat. It will take about twenty minutes longer.'

'And has Dylan got over his disapproval?' asked Brook.

I laughed. 'Yeah, but first he went round the whole house with a pair of Marigolds and some disinfectant. He can be a very prissy madam some days.'

Brook reached into her bag and pulled out a pile of magazines. 'Here. Mum was only going to throw these out. I thought we could go through them and get some ideas for decorating.'

Mum came in at that moment with a tray with mugs of tea for everybody. 'Mm, smells nice in here,' she said as she looked at the candle. 'The scent of a house is so important, isn't it? My essential oils are the first thing I unpacked so that we can get the house smelling nice.'

Mum has a gift for mixing scents – the bath lotions and potions that she makes to sell in Aunt Sarah's shop in Notting Hill are exceptional, so I knew that she would have the house smelling divine before long.

'How do you like your new home, Mrs Ruspoli?' Zahrah asked.

'We'll make it nice. There's a way to go though, and I only realised today how much stuff we need – at my sister's house we didn't need furniture, it was all there but, here, we only have the basics.'

'Freecycle,' said Zahrah. 'It's a website where people advertise stuff they don't want and you can go and get it for free. My family have got loads of stuff from there: desks, chairs, carpets, you name it. It's brilliant.'

'But why don't people want money for their things?' asked Brook.

Zahrah shrugged. 'Guess there's a lot of people out there who are into sharing and recycling.'

'My sister does something similar with clothes,' said Leela. 'Every six months or so, her and her mates do a clothes, book and CD swap evening and everyone brings along what they don't wear, or have read or don't listen to any more. She's got some fab things.'

'Could you come and show me on the computer, Zahrah?' said Mum. 'Dylan's got his computer up already and the internet seems to be working, although I'm not sure how as we haven't had our wireless system set up yet.'

'He's probably tuned into someone else's,' said Leela. 'Most people put a lock on so that no one else can use theirs, but some people don't bother.'

'I can't keep up with all this technology,' said Mum. 'But I don't think I'd like all the neighbours tapping into something I paid for.'

Mum and Zahrah went off downstairs, leaving Brook, Leela and me to pore over magazines.

By the end of the afternoon, I was feeling a hundred per cent more positive. We had some ideas for the colour scheme and decor for my room and it felt good to be designing it myself. At Aunt Sarah's, the rooms were done up to her taste, which was typically stylish and elegant and I did like it but, because it had already been done, there had been no room for me to express myself. I was looking forward to picking the colours I wanted and the fabrics and pictures for the wall that I liked. *Maybe I could do interior design as a job,* I thought, as I ripped out pages from the magazines that had caught my eye and Blu-Tacked them to the wall.

Chapter 10

Pros and Cons
of Being a Couple

'Is something the matter?' asked Joe when we drew back for breath after a snog. It was the first week back after half-term and we were sitting on the wall outside a church after school.

'No. Why?' I asked and pulled my jacket tight to keep out the cold February afternoon.

Joe shrugged. 'Oh nothing. You're a bit quiet, not your usual self, that's all.'

'I'm fine, really.' I was fine, ish, but he was right about me not being my usual self. Usually when we kissed, I was really into it but this time it was like . . . going through the motions, like my lips were kissing him but my mind was miles away and I hardly felt anything. *Does this mean I've stopped fancying him?* I wondered but, as I stared into his eyes, I felt the familiar flutter of chemistry. Phew. He had such beautiful green eyes with long curly eyelashes. *So what's the matter with me?* I wondered. 'Um. You OK?'

'Yeah, I'm great.'

'I was thinking about what we could do this weekend,' I said, in an attempt to change the subject. I felt confused by my lack of enthusiasm for kissing him because it had never happened before.

Joe smiled. 'Ah. My social secretary. So what's on the agenda then, Miss Ruspoli?'

'Dad has a team of his mates in to start the painting and decorating. He wants us to make ourselves scarce, so I thought we could do Tate Britain this time and look up the Pre-Raphaelites there. We're doing them in art history —'

While we were talking, Sam had come out of the school gates and over to join us. He gave me his usual unfriendly nod. I raised an eyebrow in acknowledgement back at him. *I can be distant too, matey,* I thought. It was a shame he was so sulky because he would be a top babe otherwise.

'Don't let me interrupt you,' he said.

'My social secretary was just giving me my itinerary,' said Joe with a grin.

'Well, don't forget we have football Saturday morning,' said Sam.

'Top of the list, wouldn't miss that,' said Joe.

'I can text you later,' I said to Joe. 'That is if you still want to go.' I didn't want to carry on with my suggestions for what we could do when Sam was there, in case he said he wanted to come along or said something sarcastic. It wouldn't be the first time. He often made sarky comments about how we were like an old married couple or we were joined at the hip and how Joe couldn't make a move any more without consulting me. That wasn't completely true, although we did wait for each other every night after school if only to see each other for ten minutes or to walk to my bus stop, but I had decided not to get into arguing with Sam. He was Joe's best mate and I had to make it work somehow.

I was about to make my excuses and go when Brook and Leela waved from the other side of the road, then came over.

'So how are our lovers?' asked Leela.

Oh God, not you too, I thought, but then I glanced at Sam. He had frozen and had gone slightly pink. I looked at Leela and Brook. Which one of them had caused the reaction? Hah! Obvious. Brook. She was staring at him with a dreamy-eyed expression and he had shifted his gaze to his shoes and looked awkward, which was a first. I was so tempted to say something but I bit my tongue. I didn't want to embarrass my mate or frighten Sam off. Not if it was love at first sight.Or was it? 'Hey, do you guys know each other?' I asked.

Sam looked back up at Brook.

'Yeah, course,' he said. 'Seen you around.'

'You too,' said Brook and their eyes locked.

'Oh get a room,' said Leela, which caused Brook to laugh like a donkey, which isn't like her, and Sam to blush even more.

'Brook, Sam, Sam, Brook,' I said.

'I've seen you in assembly,' said Sam.

'And I'm Leela, mate of India Jane's, but I get the feeling no one has even noticed I'm here.'

I put my arm around her. 'I've noticed you're here,' I said, but I knew what she was thinking: very soon she was going to be the only one of our gang of mates without a boyfriend.

On the way home, I popped in to see Aunt Sarah and see how things were progressing there since Tom and the boys had moved in during the half-term. I still had my key and found her curled up on the sofa in the front room with a book.

'What are you reading? I asked, after she'd got up to give me a warm hug.

She showed me the cover. '*Men Are from Mars, Women Are from Venus* by John Gray,' she said. 'It's so true. Men really are from another planet.'

'Tell me about it,' I said. 'How's it going?'

Aunt Sarah sighed. 'OK, early days but I guess I had got more used to being on my own than I realised, you know, having the whole double bed to myself, having my own bathroom. It's weird having to share again. Having to stay on my half of the bed, not diagonally across and he snores *and* nicks the duvet! I wake up and I think, Why am I so cold? Then I look over and there's Tom, all snuggled up with it wrapped around him double!'

I laughed. 'What about the boys? How are they doing?'

'How long have you got? Being boys, they all leave the toilet seat up and Tom leaves the cap off the toothpaste – it's going to drive me mad.'

'Why don't you say something?'

'Too soon. I want them to feel at home. Also, I don't want to go on about it, because I don't want him to think that he's moved in with an old nag.'

'Poor you. At least I haven't had living with Joe to contend with.'

'You'll have to one day – if not Joe, then some lucky chap and I can tell you, it's not always easy. There are little things you don't notice until they move in – like when Tom watches telly, he waves his foot as though listening to some imaginary music. I never noticed when we were going out but he can't sit still.'

'Joe does that. When we go to the cinema, he twitches, if it's not his foot going, it's his hands, flicking his thumb or drumming his fingers over and over.'

'And if you say anything, they get defensive.'

'Exactly,' I agreed. I curled up on the sofa opposite Aunt Sarah, happy to have her to talk to about it all. 'And if it got back to his mate Sam that I'd said anything, he'd just love that. He hates me as it is.'

'Probably jealous but, yes it is a case of love me, love my friends. And love me, love the fact that I like to lie on the sofa and watch football to relax. Honestly, India, I wish I'd given

Tom a questionnaire before he moved in – but then that's not very romantic, is it? I think we're going to have to watch TV in different rooms: me in one so I can watch my soaps, Tom somewhere else so he can watch his sport, and the boys somewhere else again so they can watch the cartoons that they're addicted to. So much for our cosy family life.'

'Are you OK, Aunt Sarah? I mean, are you having doubts that it's going to work?'

Aunt Sarah held up the book. 'I will try to *make* it work. The first year of any relationship is an adjustment. If I have learned anything from my past experiences, it is that it takes time to learn each other's ways. Time to get to a point where the silences are comfortable.'

'First *year*!' I gasped. That seemed like an awfully long time but, then again, Aunt Sarah was living with her boyfriend; Joe and I were only dating. There had to be a difference. 'So what does the book say then?'

'I'm only halfway through, but it seems to be saying that men need appreciation or they get sulky and woman need acknowledgment or they get resentful.'

'That's true,' I said. 'Like I've been doing these itineraries for Joe and me of places we can go at the weekend, partly for fun but mainly because they are related in some way to our syllabuses. It's taken a lot of time and he hasn't even said thank you. He just makes jokes about me being his social secretary.'

'And I have been making a huge effort to cook lovely meals

for Tom and the boys and, same thing, a thank you, a little gift or bunch of flowers would make all the difference but, as it is, I already feel taken for granted as chief cook and bottle washer – and I didn't sign up to a new relationship for that.'

'Exactly,' I said. 'And today for the first time, after school, Joe . . . um . . . Joe kissed me and I . . . I felt nothing, then I felt really weird and wondered if that was it, over for us. The magic gone.'

'Oh no, India, you mustn't feel that. Some days you are just preoccupied, that's all. Every relationship has its honeymoon phase when everything is brand new and you can't get enough of each other on every level. You laugh at his jokes, can't wait to see him, think his irritating habits are cute and then, a few months down the line, those little foibles you found so irresistible start to annoy you. You notice he eats too fast, sneezes too loudly —'

'Twitches his foot.'

'Exactly, and some days the kisses are wonderful and you're right back where you were those first few times and, other days, it's like, blah, get out of my face and pick your dirty socks up from the floor while you're at it.'

I cracked up.

'Some days I feel I love Tom to bits, other days I feel independent, irritable and he's just another annoying bloke, and what was I doing moving in with him so fast?'

'So why did you do it? Why do I do it?'

81

'Yes. Why do we? Companionship. Love. Friendship. I don't know, India, but don't you worry if you have days when you feel like you've gone off Joe, in fact some days you will probably down-right dislike him. It doesn't mean that the relationship is over. It just means that it's getting real. Is Joe your first proper boyfriend?'

I nodded.

'OK, then days like this are a good learning curve for you, because it's only after that first flush that you begin to really see if you are suited to each other. If you can work through the days when one of you is moody, days when you feel flat when you kiss each other, days when you have your period and everyone annoys you, days when he sees you at your worst and days when you see him at his. Part of being in a grown-up relationship is not jumping ship the moment the rose-tinted glasses come off.'

'I guess,' I said. 'Doesn't feel very romantic though, does it?'

Aunt Sarah laughed. 'No. Toilet seats left up, toothpaste without the cap on is about as far from romance as you can get, but it's what makes up day-to-day living.'

'So when do you know it's over?'

'When you are more miserable than happy. When the days he annoys you far outweigh the days you love or like him. Percentages, I guess.'

It felt good to be having a girlie chat with Aunt Sarah and bonding over the ups and downs of being in a new relationship. I felt she understood more than Mum, who had been besotted with Dad for ever and vice versa. By the time I left, I felt a lot better about Joe. Days like this were all part of the rollercoaster of being in a proper grown-up relationship.

When I got home, I went to my computer to check if there were any messages. On the list, I noticed that there was one from Bruno. He was a boy who I had known all my life but hadn't seen for years until my gran's birthday last year in Ravello. We had a holiday romance but broke it off soon after, partly because of Joe and partly because it didn't seem to make sense to have a long distance-relationship so early on in my dating life. I clicked on his name and read the screen.

Ciao bella,
Am in London for a few days in April. Would love to see you.
Are you free on the Saturday before the Easter weekend?
Bruno.
XX

I really wanted to see him. We'd had the most mega romantic time in Italy and a fab date in London before deciding not to take it any further. It had been a funny time because, after months of no boys, three babes had come along all at the same time: Bruno, Tyler and Joe – and I'd had to decide. I had picked Joe, but that didn't mean that I didn't feel something for all of them. They were all so different. Bruno made me feel like a princess and being with him felt so sophisticated. I felt admiration for Tyler, like I could learn a lot by hanging out with him but, with Joe, I felt most myself, like we were on the same wavelength.

I remembered how Joe had been when he'd seen me with Tyler. *How would he be if I met up with Bruno?* I wondered. *Or shouldn't I tell him?* What he didn't know, wouldn't worry him. As I wondered how to reply to Bruno, I felt frustrated that I wasn't free to do what I wanted. A day with Bruno. I needn't snog him. There would be nothing in it – just two old friends catching up and he had been a friend of the family since I was tiny. I decided to take the risk. See Bruno. Not tell Joe. I didn't have to tell him my every move, it wasn't as if we were married and, anyway, he usually played football on Saturday mornings so wouldn't want to see me anyway. I quickly typed my reply.

Great timing. Love to see you. Let me know what time and where.
Ciao yourself.
India Jane.

I pressed the send button before I could change my mind and off the message went.

Chapter 11

Out and About

'I don't know if I've ever really said this before, but I think that you are the best-looking boy in our school and I love spending time with you,' I said to Joe as we stood waiting to do the London tourist open-topped bus ride at Green Park on Saturday afternoon.

'Are you on drugs?' he asked.

I shook my head. I had remembered what Aunt Sarah had said about boys needing appreciation and I was determined to give it a go. 'And you're a great kisser, too,' I said.

Joe laughed. 'You are definitely on drugs,' he said, but he took my hand and I could see that he was chuffed. *Result,* I thought and made a mental note to let Aunt Sarah know.

I had worked out a great itinerary for us again, up to and even including Easter. The first Saturday of April I had saved for Bruno and had to find an excuse to give to Joe as to why I wouldn't be around. I had been in touch a few times with Bruno since his first email. He would be over visiting an uncle who managed a serviced apartment block in Knightsbridge and he wanted to see how it worked and whether it was a venture that might work back in Italy. Hotel management was to be his career and he did a lot of work experience as part of his course. I was looking forward to seeing him again, not only because he was great company but also because he was another one to talk prospective careers over with.

'What have you got planned for us for the holidays?' asked Joe, as if he had picked up on my thoughts.

'Few exhibitions,' I said. 'I'll email you the details. And I'd like to do one of the boat trips. Greenwich or Hampton Court.'

'Hampton Court,' said Joe. 'I want to go there to take some photos for my portfolio. I want to focus on the river and get as many shots as I can from different locations.'

'Good idea,' I said. I had seen some of the photos he had taken the day we were down by the river when we'd been to Tate Modern and they were fabulous. 'And can I take some photos of you for my art project?'

Joe nodded. My portraits of friends idea was going great, but I hadn't done any of Joe yet. I was looking forward to getting some photos of him and then working on them in the darkroom at school. It would be fun playing around with his image and seeing how I could change it or distort it. I had had an idea of doing a collage of some photos of him, making some light and some dark to show the different aspects of having a boyfriend – like the sunny days when everything felt great and the shadow days when it was harder work.

'Everyone on,' called a man from the bus company as the bus doors opened and people began to pile on.

'Shall we go up top?' asked Joe. 'Will you be warm enough?'

I nodded. It was a dry day and I had a fleece on under my jacket and a hat in case it got windy. Once up top, we took the back seat where Joe put his arm around me. 'We can snuggle up if we get cold,' he said. 'And, er . . . back at you, what you said before we got on the bus. Have I ever told you that I think you're really pretty? Um, I do rate you . . . a lot.'

'Thank you,' I said. 'No. You haven't ever told me and it is nice to hear.' *Wow*, I thought, the appreciation thing really did work! We'd both made each other feel really good.

We sat with our arms wrapped around each other as the bus started up and began to make its way down Piccadilly towards Hyde Park corner.

We could only just make out what the bus guide was saying about Green Park and St James's Park and Buckingham Palace, but neither of us wanted to move closer to him because it was nice being on the back row together away from everyone else.

'So, going back to the hols,' said Joe, as we chugged on

around the roundabout and began to head back up Piccadilly. 'How about we take a boat to Hampton Court on the first Saturday morning in April?'

'I . . . Oh. Um. No. I can't do that Saturday. Can you do Sunday?'

'I'd rather do Saturday.'

'What about football?'

'Coach is away so it's been cancelled. Why, is there a problem?'

'Yes. No. Not a problem, just I . . . I can't do it.'

'OK. Why not?'

I felt myself going red as I desperately scrabbled around in my head trying to think what to tell him. The truth? No. He might go off on a jealousy trip. Cancel Bruno? No. I wanted to see him. 'Um. Family thing.'

'What family thing? You never said. Am I invited?'

'Yes. No. Um. An old family friend is over from Ravello and wants to meet up.'

'That's where your dad's from, isn't it?'

'It's where my gran still lives. She's got a fab house there.'

'So am I invited?'

'Um. Not sure.'

Joe took his arm away from my shoulder and was quiet for a while. It felt uncomfortable, like the conversation wasn't over but neither of us was saying what we needed to say.

'I'll find out from Dad,' I said after a few minutes.

Joe shrugged a shoulder. 'It's OK. I . . . I just thought you liked me coming to your family dos, that's all. Doesn't matter. I can find something else to do.'

I'd hurt him. I could tell.

'No. No. Course, you know Dad loves you and we love having you around, even if the place has been in a mess lately with all the decorating going on.' The house was more than a mess with paint pots and brushes all over the hall and what furniture we had shoved into the corners and covered with sheets in most of the rooms.

'So will it be ready in time for your family do, then?'

I shrugged. 'Er . . . maybe. Probably, the way that Dad is going at it.'

Neither of us said anything for a while and we watched the passing sights and traffic.

'So come on, what's up, Ruspoli?' asked Joe after a few minutes.

'Nothing. I . . . just assumed you had other plans, that's all. That's why I didn't mention it.'

Joe was quiet again and we both strained to listen to what the guide was saying. Something about the Great Fire of London being started in a baker's shop and destroying most of the City of London. I reached over and took Joe's hand.

'I'd still like to do Hampton Court, just not that Saturday,' I said. 'And Greenwich, too. Maybe later in the hols. My mates went a few weeks ago and said it's fab.'

'I know, you said last week but I've already been there,' said Joe.

'Oh. OK. Does that mean that you don't want to go again?'

Joe shrugged. *Oh God,* I thought. *This isn't going well. He's upset with me.* I decided to plunge in.

'Are you mad with me?'

Joe laughed. 'No. Why would I be mad with you?'

'Don't know. Our plans for the hols? Hampton Court? Don't you want to do it now? You have to say. We could go at Easter weekend instead? What do you think? Don't just go along with me.'

'I do want to go,' said Joe. 'Just . . . I . . . Oh, I'll tell you later but don't pencil in a boat trip for that weekend as I have something I want to do.'

'What?'

'Later. Can't tell you now.'

I felt myself getting cross with him. Was he playing tit for tat? Because I was being mysterious about the first Saturday, was he getting back at me?

He put his hand over mine and patted it. 'All is cool, Ruspoli,' he said.

All is not cool, Joe, I thought. *I'd like to thump you.* But I didn't say anything.

'It's true though,' Joe continued. 'I'm not that bothered about doing Greenwich again.'

'We can do something else that we both want to do,' I suggested.

'Maybe, hey, don't get me wrong, most of the time I'm happy to go along with what you want to do —'

'*I* want to do?' I echoed. 'No. I thought you wanted to as well.'

Joe frowned. 'Not really. I mean, I like hanging out with you and I don't really mind where we do it. It was your idea to incorporate these sightseeing trips into our time together.'

'Yes. For homework. Our projects. I thought it would make it more fun.'

Joe nodded. 'As I said, your idea.'

I was feeling more and more uncomfortable. 'Are you saying I am bossy?'

Joe grinned. 'All girls are bossy, given half the chance.'

'Hey, that's not fair. I'm not bossy. I thought we were doing what we both wanted.'

'But you never exactly asked me, did you?'

'Yes I did. I *did*. I asked if you wanted to do the things on the list.'

'Yes, you asked me that and, yes, I do want to do most of them. Why not? But what you never asked is what *I* would like to be on the list. Where I would like to go. My first choice sometimes.'

'OK, so what would *you* want to be on the list?' I asked. I felt like my voice was getting shaky.

Joe put his hand on my arm. 'Hey, India Jane, chill. Don't get upset.'

When he said that, part of me felt totally upset. 'What is going on here?' I asked. 'Are we having a row? Are you telling me you don't like what has been going on? I'm trying to

91

understand and now you're telling me to chill.'

'All I'm saying is that it would have been nice to have put things on the list that we *both* wanted to do, to decide our itinerary together, not just what you wanted to do. But it's not a big deal, no need to make it into one.'

Arghhhh. I felt like screaming. 'Me make it into a big deal? It's you who doesn't like what's going on. I spent ages on the computer, you know, working out trips and finding out opening times and looking for things that we could do that would be free or wouldn't cost much.'

'Great. But I never asked you to do that and I would have done some of it as well if you'd let me, and you're right, some of it is stuff related to coursework. And yeah, it's nice to see London as a tourist like today. You're right. I should see more of the city we live in.'

'Yes, but do you want to? I want you to be happy.'

'I am. I'm cool.'

Argh. Argh. Argh. 'OK. So what would you like to do? We'll do exactly what you want one weekend.'

'I wouldn't lay that on you, India Jane. I can be a lazy bugger. I like lying about listening to music on my iPod. I like playing football. I like watching sport. See. I can tell by your face that doesn't turn you on, which is why I haven't dragged you along to anything.'

'Meaning I have dragged you along.'

I felt like getting off the bus. We both sat there with our arms crossed over our chests. This was so not the fabbie-dabbie day out that I had planned. *I know nothing about relationships,* I thought, as the bus approached St Paul's Cathedral on our left, *and I think I need another session with Aunt Sarah and her Mars and Venus book fast.*

Chapter 12

House into a Home

Back at the house, the efforts of team Ruspoli and friends were
beginning to show.

On Zahrah's advice, Mum had explored the recycling
websites, plus she'd found a row of second-hand furniture shops
on the main road near the house. Just about every night that we'd
got home from school over the last few weeks, Dad and some of
his mates from the orchestra or Ethan and Lewis had been round
to help with the painting and often there was another one of
Mum's 'finds' in the hallway – a fireplace, chairs, chest of drawers,
mirrors or door frames. To begin with, it had looked like junk,
then she would describe what she was going to do with a piece
and within days it would begin to be transformed.

One night I came home to find an old pine wardrobe cluttering up the hallway. 'I thought we could rub it down, paint it white, then apply streaks of silver-grey paint effect to the edges to get the look of old French furniture,' she said.

I got what she meant immediately and bagged it and a chest of drawers that had been deposited in the kitchen the night before to go with it. I was beginning to see that, with a bit of imagination, we could transform anything. We didn't need loads of dosh, just an idea and a paintbrush. I decided to do my room in a soft pale blue and all the furniture, doors and woodwork in the white-paint effect, plus Aunt Sarah had given me the most divine dove-grey silk bedspread as a house-warming present. It was going to look so elegant. On the wall, I decided to hang just one poster, a black and white shot of Audrey Hepburn from the movie *Breakfast at Tiffany's*. It was a house-warming present from Joe after we'd been to see it one Saturday afternoon at an art cinema in Notting Hill that showed old films.

I liked having mementos of our time together and to have the poster on the wall meant more than just a picture in a frame. It would forever remind me of sitting in the cinema, holding hands and snogging Joe. Neither of us had mentioned the first Saturday in April again, so I presumed that he was cool with it and had made other plans for that day. I think Mum and Dad were feeling the same way about decorating the house as I was and they had even more mementos from their life together and all the places we had lived. All their things had been packed away when we were at Aunt Sarah's and it was lovely to see familiar items and artefacts from my childhood reappear. The downstairs hall and living room were designated our Indian area and were painted red with orange ceilings, then Mum and Dad unearthed the stuff that they'd bought in India that had been in boxes for ages – gorgeous silk paintings of Indian princes, old faded photos of Indian families that Dad said he had taken in Rajasthan. The kitchen was painted in the sunny colours of St Lucia in the Caribbean; a huge green, red, blue and yellow toy parrot was perched in the corner on top of a dresser (the parrot used to belong to Dylan, but he denies all knowledge of it) and Mum found some discounted red and yellow crockery in Portobello Road which was from Portugal. It went perfectly and the whole room was a riot of colour, great for getting you 'in that get up and go mood' in the morning as Dad said every breakfast time until we had to tell him to get up and go, like really, gooooooo away, Dad.

The bathroom was white with turquoise and silver candleholders from Essaouria in Morocco. Mum put her sandalwood and jasmine bath products in and soon the damp smell that had been there was replaced with a lovely exotic scent of flowers and herbs. Mum and Dad's bedroom was the Italian room. They painted the walls a deep fuchsia pink and, on one wall, they had put a floor to ceiling hanging that showed a scene of the landscape around Tuscany. Dad said that it had been in his family for centuries. I vaguely remembered it from when we lived in Italy, but it must have been folded away for the last few years. Aunt Sarah had bought them a six-foot-high mirror with an ornate silver frame. It made the room look twice the size. At the windows were plush, purple velvet curtains that Mum had bought in Ireland in a garage sale and she had found a matching velvet bedspread in Camden Lock. In the corner was a life-size Roman statue of a naked man with his arm missing that Dad had found in a salvage yard in Willesden. The room looked decadent and opulent and I was beginning to see that my parents really did have a flair for design.

Dylan's room was the only neutral room. He wanted it white with one blue wall and no knick-knacks. He declared the rest of the house as OTT, insane and an embarrassment should he ever bring a friend home. 'Which I won't,' he said.

I loved it. I loved walking around and seeing evidence of all the places I had lived and, although I had liked living in Aunt Sarah's, I realised that it had always been her home with her things and that this house was more where I truly belonged.

'And hardly cost us much,' said Dad, after we had given Joe the tour one day when everything was finished and in its place. 'Just the paint which we got from a trade place up in North London. Most of the stuff we can take with us if and when we find a place to buy.'

'When will that be then?' asked Dylan. 'I can't wait, although I expect you will go mad with the paint pots and the junk shop rubbish there too.'

'Looks great, Mr Ruspoli,' said Joe. 'And nice that it will all be ready for your family day in the Easter holidays.'

'Family day? What family day?' asked Dad and I felt a wave of panic hit me. My initial reaction was to run but I couldn't. Instead I went the colour of Mum and Dad's new bedroom. Deep fuchsia.

'Oh you know,' Joe continued, 'India Jane mentioned it – some of your friends are coming over from Ravello, aren't they?'

Dad looked puzzled. 'Are they? Who?' he asked. 'No one tells me anything.'

Joe looked at me. 'Maybe I got it wrong? Old friends of the family or something?'

'I . . . oh . . .' I blustered.

'Oh you mean Bruno,' said Dylan. 'Remember, Dad? Bruno's coming over, but *we're* not having a family day with him. India Jane's going to see him though, aren't you?'

All eyes turned to me. 'Oh yes, Bruno. I . . . I'm sure I mentioned him to you. I knew him when I was a kid. He lives near my nanna in Ravello.'

Joe stiffened ever so slightly. 'Really? Hmm. Don't remember you telling me about a Bruno when you showed me the photos from your visit there.'

Chapter 13

If Only

If only.

If only I had been honest.

If only I had *told* Bruno I had a boyfriend.

If only I had told Joe that I had told Bruno that I had a boyfriend. I could even have invited Joe along to meet him. (Yeah right. That would be fun. Not.)

If only I hadn't lied and said it was a family thing on the first Saturday in April.

If only I wasn't such a coward.

If *only* Mum and Dad hadn't been sifting through photos from Ravello looking for a nice family one to put in a frame the day before Joe was over. I hadn't realised they were out on the table when he came round until it was too late. He casually asked if Bruno was in any of the shots and went very quiet when he saw what a total love god Bruno was.

Now it was a million times worse than it would have been if I'd only told the truth from the beginning.

My list of things to remember when having a relationship was growing:

- Try and like his mates.
- Learn to put myself in his shoes if he seems to overreact to a situation.
- Listen to his point of view.
- Don't try to take over and be his social secretary. He won't thank me for it.
- Be honest. *Most* of all, be honest.

'Have you seen him since?' asked Leela.

I shook my head. It was Monday morning break at school and I'd been hanging around outside the Sixth Form common room in the hope that Joe might come out and I could try and make amends, though I didn't know how I was going to react if I did see him. I'd spent all night tossing and turning and trying to work out what to say or do.

Apologise? 'I'm new at this, Joe. This is my first proper relationship and I am still learning the rules.' Maybe.

Stand my ground. 'We're not married. You don't own me. I don't have to tell you everything I do.' Maybe too aggressive and

Joe might get defensive.

Declare my feelings and wrap myself around his ankles until he forgives me. Maybe too desperate.

Wrestle him to the ground and tickle him until he laughs and forgets it all. Yeah right, like that's going to happen.

Tell him I was struck by lightning and was experiencing temporary insanity. Not a bad idea but unlikely he'd believe me.

'Any suggestions of how I should play it, guys?' I asked. 'I'm all out of ideas.'

'Come clean,' said Zahrah. 'Tell him that, after the way he reacted when he saw you with Tyler, you didn't want to go through that again.'

'Yeah, but he did apologise and we did make up,' I said and, when I remembered how ardent his kisses had been, that option suddenly had appeal.

'What happened when he realised that you were going to meet a boy?' asked Leela.

'It was awful. Mum and Dad got it immediately – that I wanted to see Bruno and not tell Joe. Don't forget they were there in Ravello last year too, and saw us together. Mum knows how much I liked him, but they've always told me to be honest. I think they were torn between wanting to protect me and being cross that I clearly hadn't told Joe the truth. They went into an overdrive act of offering tea, clearing up the Ravello photos on the table as if removing the evidence, offering to show Joe the garden, anything to divert attention away from me and my scarlet face. Afterwards, Dad said he was disappointed in me. I said he didn't have to be because I was disappointed in myself.'

'Oh poor India Jane,' said Leela and she put her arm around me.

'How did Joe leave it?' asked Brook.

'He didn't hang around. He left soon after. No kiss. No text later. No nothing.'

'Have you contacted him?' asked Zahrah.

I shook my head. 'I want to, I just don't know what to say.'

At that moment, I saw Sam come out of the common room. He clocked Brook straight away and came over.

'Where's Joe?' asked Leela. Sometimes I can't believe her! Subtlety is not one of her strong points.

Sam shrugged. 'Haven't seen him. Why?' he asked, then looked at me. 'I thought you knew his every move.'

'I . . . er . . .' I so didn't want Sam to know what had happened in case he gloated. 'Yeah. Course. I saw him yesterday.'

'I'm having a party on Friday night,' Brook blurted. 'Want to come?'

I breathed a sigh of relief when I saw that Sam was going into flirt mode and wasn't going to goad me about Joe.

'Maybe,' he said. 'Who is going to be there?'

Brook was so cool, it was brilliant and, when she secretly winked at me, I realised that she had seen how uncomfortable I was and was distracting him. She didn't reply immediately. 'Who is going to be there? Well, not my mum. She's going to the theatre with a bunch of friends. And . . . I wasn't planning on a big party. VIPs only, so that would leave, me and . . .' She took a step closer to him and slowly raised her eyes up to his, 'you.'

Leela raised an eyebrow at me.

'Sounds like a party to me,' Sam said in a throaty voice. He was well hooked. I wanted to laugh. *Like, way to go Brook,* I thought. *Result.*

'God, it's getting hot around here,' said Zahrah, and she made a motion as if fanning herself. We all cracked up, even Sam.

After he'd gone, Brook grinned at us. 'I saw someone do that in a movie,' she said. 'I've been dying to try it out.'

'Impressive,' said Leela, then her face fell. 'But you know what this means? I am going to be the only singleton. It's the Easter hols next week and, India, you'll be with Joe —'

'You don't know that. He hates me.'

'You'll make it up. He's so into you, anyone can see that. He's not going to roll over and let some Italian boy swan in and take you off him, even if Bruno is a love god. Joe's probably planning some great romantic come-back as we speak.'

'Yeah right,' I said. Joe was lovely, but so far he hadn't been big on the romantic gestures, that was for sure. His style was to be cool.

'And you will be with Sam,' Leela continued to Brook.

'Not necessarily,' she said, then she grinned. 'Although it is just a matter of time.'

103

'Exactly,' said Leela. 'And you, Zahrah, you've got Ryan.'

Zahrah nodded. 'And we have got a lot of plans for over Easter, it's true, but hey Leela, you know you're always welcome to —'

'To tag along like a great gooseberry? No thanks. I shall stay at home, in my bedroom with the blinds down, listening to sad songs about loneliness and being single . . .' She pulled such a sad face and, even though I knew she was messing about playing the clown, I could tell that there was an element of truth behind it all. I remembered how I had felt when I first came to London, before I had my new mates, and my cousin Kate was always out and about with her boyfriend, and I had no one to hang out with.

'OK, how about this?' I said. 'Come with me to meet Bruno on Saturday. You wouldn't be tagging along because we're not a couple, he's not my boyfriend —'

'Brilliant plan,' said Zahrah. 'And you can tell Joe that Leela is going with you, India Jane. He can't get too possessive knowing that you have a chaperone.'

Leela rolled her eyes. 'You make it sound like I'm a character out of Jane Austen, but really, could I come along?'

'Course,' I said and I meant it, but I also felt a sinking feeling that I wouldn't get any time alone with Bruno after all.

After school, I went to Starbucks and bought a block of cinnamon chocolate. My dad has called me Cinnamon Girl since

I was born. Partly because of my colouring; my coppery hair and my eyes are amber – the colour of cinnamon spice Dad says, and partly because one of his favourite songs is by Neil Young and is called 'Cinnamon Girl'. Just before Christmas, I bought a bar of the chocolate for Joe and then got it all over my teeth, which wasn't a good look, but the day I gave it to him was the beginning of something because soon afterwards we got together.

I went around to his house armed with my peace offering. I knew that he was there, because I had got Leela to call straight after school and see if he picked up – which he did. Of course, we dialled 141 first so that, if he was there and rang the number back to see who the last caller was, he wouldn't know who it was, although when he answered the phone, Leela disguised her voice and went into a mad act pretending to be someone calling to sell kitchen design. That girl can be bonkers at times. I hope he didn't realise it was her.

Five o'clock on the dot, I rang his doorbell.

His mum, Charlotte, had her hair wrapped up in a towel when she opened the door. 'Hi India Jane, go on up.' 'Scuse the look, wet hair,' she said and let me past.

Before I could lose my nerve, I raced up the stairs and knocked on the door.

'Yep,' said Joe.

'It's me.'

A few moments later, the door opened and Joe stood aside to let me in.

I went in and sat on the end of the bed. 'OK. I . . . I want to explain about Bruno.'

Joe put up his hand. 'Look, before we go any further, I have something I want to say to you. This thing, you know, you, me. If you want out, India Jane, I want you to say so. I don't believe in staying with someone if you want to move on or if you're feeling trapped or whatever. Believe me, I've been there and it's not nice. So. If you want to be free, I understand. No one would understand better than me. If you want to date other boys, fine. We can still —'

'Be friends?' I finished for him.

Joe smiled. 'Yeah. I think we could.'

I felt a wave of sadness come over me as I looked at him sitting there in his jeans and black T-shirt, the slight curve of muscle on his upper arms, his hair in need of a cut and those beautiful green eyes with the circle of blue around the iris. No mistaking, he was gorgeous and I still fancied him like mad. I so didn't want to break up with him.

'Friends?' I asked.

He nodded. 'If that's what you want.'

'What do you want?'

'I don't know. Win the lottery. Get a publishing deal to go to India and take photos. Five A-star A-levels.'

'You know what I mean.'

Joe took my hand. 'I do. I want you to be happy and I want to be in a relationship where I can trust the person I'm with.

This Bruno thing, I just wish you'd told me the truth. I mean, hey, I know we both have pasts, have dated other people, fancied other people. I would naïve to think you hadn't.'

I decided to follow Zahrah's advice and go for the truth. 'Exactly. I wish I'd told you the truth. I am so sorry, Joe, I can't tell you. All I can say is I am new to this relationship thing and I know I messed up big time. I made a mistake, I did, but I regret it. I do. I don't want to break up with you and be your friend. I don't. I do want to see Bruno though. I've known him a long time and OK, yeah, we did have a few moments back there, but it's over. I mean, he lives in Italy and I'm here, but also . . . there's another reason that I didn't tell you the truth. After Tyler that time, I didn't want to upset you . . .'

'Yeah. I know I was out of order that time. And of course boys are going to find you attractive,' he said, then grinned. 'Poor Tyler, I bet he was gutted when he found out you were with me. You're stunning, India Jane, and you're fun to be with. Boys are always going to look at you and I realise I have to deal with it, but you have to tell me the truth about what you want and what is really going on with you.'

'Deal. OK. Truth. Bruno is coming over. I do want to see him. I want to be friends with him. Come too, if you want.'

Joe shrugged. 'I can't now. I told Sam and Chris I'd hang out.'

'Leela's coming.'

'Leela?'

'Yeah. She's the only one of us without a boyfriend and I

promised I'd introduce her to Bruno.'

Joe grinned again. 'Now *that* I like the sound of. But Brook, she's single isn't she?'

'Not for long, I think. She and Sam are having a private party on Friday night.'

Joe raised an eyebrow.

'If we're being honest Joe, can I ask something else?'

'Shoot.'

'No games with us.'

'No games? Meaning?'

'Meaning – when I was mysterious about Bruno, you said you had something you might be doing at Easter weekend, like you were playing games, tit for tat sort of thing, getting back at me by being secretive.'

'Not a game,' said Joe. 'OK. I guess this is a good time to tell you. You have been so good about trying to work out things for us to do, I thought I'd return the favour. Easter weekend. A trip away. My mum asked your parents already because I wanted it to be a surprise, and they said it would be OK as long as I didn't pounce on you and I promised not to, least not any more than usual.'

'Trip away? Where to?'

'Bath. Loads to do, see. Another river for me to photograph. Maybe even paint. My uncle and aunt live there and had invited Mum and Dad and me to go, so I asked if you could come as well. They said you'd be very welcome if you'd like to join us and Mum is cool with it, too. Dad's not coming. He's got to stay in London and catch up on work. If you come, it means Mum can do her own thing. What do you think?'

'Bath? Yes. Fab. I've always wanted to go there. And you might have promised not to pounce on me, but I haven't promised not to pounce on you.' I pushed him back and slid next to him to kiss him. As he leaned forward to kiss me back, I thought, *I must remember this in the future. I think I know what people are thinking sometimes, but actually, I don't. I really, really don't know what goes on in anybody else's head. So much of it, my imagination makes up. The truth is a lot more fun.*

Chapter 14

Bruno

'I so thought Joe was through with me,' I said to Leela as we came out of the tube station at Tottenham Court Road, 'but actually I'd projected what I was imagining in my head on to him. Like, I thought he was mad with me or would want to break up, and all the time he'd been planning this lovely trip.'

'So he did come through with the romantic gesture in the end, then?' she replied, as she got out her umbrella to shield us from a shower. 'I thought you said that he wasn't big on romance.'

'I know and that wasn't fair. I'd forgotten at Christmas he did a compilation CD for me, mainly love songs and one of the tracks was 'Cinnamon Girl' by Neil Young. That was romantic I guess.'

'*Yeah*. That is so sweet. Most boys wouldn't ever think of

doing something like that and you can keep the CD for ever,' she said.

I nodded. I realised that I had been taking Joe for granted lately, forgetting how lovely he could be sometimes, but yesterday it felt like we were back on track and things were as good as they had ever been, plus we had our first trip away together to look forward to. I couldn't wait.

Leela and I had both made an effort with our appearances for Bruno, and Leela looked gorgeous with her hair loose down her back. She was wearing a cropped grey military jacket from Topshop and jeans and high boots. She looked stylish, sophisticated, and I could see boys checking her out as we looked for Bruno. I was also wearing my jeans and had borrowed Mum's peacock-blue velvet coat and pale-blue scarf because she said it complemented my colouring. I was looking forward to spending some time with Bruno, partly for his company and partly because he made me feel so good about myself – like I was the only girl on the planet in his eyes.

'There he is,' I said, as I spotted Bruno waiting by a newspaper stall. He was wearing his brown winter coat and a huge red scarf wrapped a few times around his neck. He turned and saw me and I felt my stomach flip. He was looking more handsome than I had remembered and stood out in the crowd with his Italian good looks.

He gave me a huge bear hug when we got to him and kissed Leela's hand when I introduced them. She blushed and looked very coy — which is most unlike Leela because she is usually confident and cheeky around boys. While we walked along, we chatted about what we had been up to and I could see that he and Leela had instantly clicked and I couldn't help wishing that I had Bruno to myself. *But you have a boyfriend,* I told myself. *You have Joe.*

We had decided to go to the British Museum and look at an exhibition of paintings from Jodphur in Rajasthan. I had read about the exhibition in Dad's Sunday paper and I remembered that Bruno liked looking at art.

'Have you ever been to India?' he asked Leela when we reached the museum and headed inside.

'I was there last summer,' she replied as I indicated to go on to the centre to get our tickets. 'My grandmother is still over there in Jaipur.'

'Jaipur? Isn't that also in Rajasthan, like Jodphur?'

Leela nodded.

'I've seen travel brochures, I've always wanted to go there,' said Bruno.

'You should. It's wonderful and utterly insane at the same time,' said Leela. 'Like, on the roads, you can be driving along and it's common to see an elephant stroll past or a family of pigs, hens, a camel, and then six men will ride past hanging off the back of a moped, and the number of people they get on one bus has to be seen to be believed, like people up on the roof as well as packed inside. The place is so alive. Buzzing. Some of the houses there are beautiful. Lots of the original ones have been turned into hotels, but my grandmother managed to keep hers. It's been in the family for a long time.'

'Sounds fascinating,' said Bruno, and I could see that he was really looking at her, not just listening but looking with appreciation. 'My father's house in Italy has also been with the same family for many centuries. It has such a sense of history there.'

'I lived in Rajasthan too,' I said, not wanting to be left out of the conversation. 'In Udaipur.'

Bruno nodded. 'Yes, I know.'

'I thought you were born there,' said Leela, 'but didn't actually live there for any length of time.'

'Born, lived. Born, that's what I meant.'

'Have you been back?' asked Bruno.

I shook my head.

'Do you remember it at all?' asked Leela.

I shook my head again. They were both looking at me expectantly and I was beginning to feel stupid. I had nothing more to add. 'Um. Mum and Dad remember it, of course. They have loads of stuff from there. We've put some silk paintings and photographs from there up in our new house.'

'I know,' said Leela. 'I was there last week, don't forget. You showed me.'

'Yeah, I know. Um. I love Indian food . . . er, curry. Don't you?' I asked and they both nodded and Leela gave me a strange look, like I was off my head. I felt even more stupid. I wished I'd come on my own with Bruno and then I could have shown off *my* knowledge of India, limited though it was, instead of Leela.

'Jaipur is also the best place to buy gems,' Leela continued, 'so take some dosh with you if you go, Bruno, so you can buy something for the lady in your life.' She gave him another coy look.

'No lady at the moment,' said Bruno with a quick glance at me, then he grinned. 'Work, work, work.'

Leela grinned back and looked up into his eyes. 'I'm sure that won't be for long.'

I couldn't believe it. Major flirting was happening right under my nose. Major flirting with *my* Bruno. My *ex*-boyfriend but even so! We got to the ticket area where Bruno insisted on paying for our tickets.

He handed us one each. 'My treat. And I believe that Jaipur is also famous for the tailoring,' he said as he linked arms with Leela and beckoned me to follow them. 'When I finally make it over there, maybe you could recommend places for me to go. You must give me your email before we part.'

'Sure,' said Leela. 'Anything you need to know, just get in touch.'

I trudged after them feeling like a sulky teenager. Which is exactly what I was. Last time I had seen him, I had felt like a princess. *His* princess. Now I felt like lady-in-waiting to

Princess Leela — no, even worse, I wasn't that, I wasn't even the lady-in-waiting, I was the lady-in-the-way, the gooseberry.

I must make an effort to join in, I thought, and walked faster so that I caught up with them. I couldn't believe it. I heard him ask if Leela was seeing anyone.

'No,' she said and looked at him coyly.

'How about you, India Jane?' he asked.

'Mfnf,' came out of my mouth. Bruno was looking at me as if waiting for an answer. I didn't know what to say. Bruno was my ex. We'd had a connection in Italy. Surely he didn't want to hear that I was blissfully in love with another boy? *Another question for Aunt Sarah,* I thought to myself. How to deal with exes?

'Mff, yes, Joe . . . we have a lot in common. We go to the same school, too. Who wants some water? I might go to the shop before we go in,' I blurted.

'No thanks,' chorused Bruno and Leela, then they both laughed. *Grrr,* I thought as I turned to go back to get my water. *How comfy cosy are they?*

When I reached the shop, Leela caught up with me. 'Er, I told Bruno I wanted some mints. Look. Is this OK with you?' she asked. 'Because I think he likes me.'

'Yeah. Course,' I said, and made myself smile through gritted teeth. 'I think he does, too.' Inside, I felt like my brain was about to explode. It wasn't OK, but I knew it would look mean if I said so. I knew I couldn't lay claim to him. He was single. Leela was single. I was the one happy happy with my boyfriend, wasn't I?

I went into the shop, bought water and mints then went back to join them in the exhibition. They were standing in front of a fabulous painting of a herd of flying elephants and they seemed very comfortable with each other, chatting away like they'd known each other for ever. I trailed after them feeling more and more like I was in the way and, even though the paintings were wonderful and colourful, I didn't enjoy being there. After half an hour, Leela went off to find the Ladies and I was alone with Bruno at last.

'You're friend is cute,' he said. 'And very bright, so easy to talk to. I . . . um, well, you know I am over on my own and I wondered, would you mind if I took her out while I am here?'

Whadddddddt? Take HER OUT? No WAY, said a voice in my head. *You're mine, mine, MINE.*

'No, course not, why should I mind?' said a voice that came out of my mouth.

'You are a fantastic girl, India Jane. So cool. That's what I always liked about you. Some girls can be so irrational and possessive,' he said and took my hand. 'It can be a bit lonely sometimes when I travel, so it would be lovely to have someone like Leela to hang out with. I was going to ask you but now, well, I wouldn't want to tread on Jake —'

'Joe.'

'— Joe's toes.'

116

Knickers, said the voice in my head. *Blooming bloomin' knickers.* I liked Joe. I really did, but sometimes having a boyfriend really put the kibosh on things.

Leela came back from the Ladies and we did the rest of the exhibition. I walked around with them, we bought postcards of the paintings that we liked in the museum shop and, as I watched them flirt away, I couldn't help but think, *How in the heckity hoolah did this happen? How come all of a sudden, I am the odd one out?*

We came out of the museum after an hour or so and my phone bleeped that I had a text. It was from Joe.

How's it going with Bruno?

Gr8, I texted back. *He sms 2 lke Leela. Lv is in the air.*

He texted back. *Fantastic.*

No, not fantastic, I thought.

You are not a nice girl, said one of the voices in my head.

I don't care, said another. *Bruno is mine. Was mine. So is Tyler. And so are all the boys in the whole world, mine mine mine.*

'I am going mad,' I said out loud and a white-haired lady who was passing smiled.

'Aren't we all, dear?' she said.

Chapter 15

Boy in Bath

'Here we are,' said Joe's mum when we got to the end of a lane at the top of a steep hill behind the train station in Bath. In front of us was a Georgian town house with a wrought-iron veranda and garden at the front.

'It's so pretty,' I said. 'Feels like the middle of the country although it's in town.'

Joe got out and opened the car door for me. I had been really looking forward to our trip because, even though there would be grown-ups around, Joe's mum had made it clear that she was happy for Joe and me to go off on our own. I had spent an hour or two researching Bath on the internet and I knew it was going to be the most romantic weekend ever. Three whole days with

Joe. Heaven. After my day out with Bruno, I'd reminded myself how lucky I was to have Joe, and I had given myself a severe telling off about being so jealous of Leela and him liking each other. I had a fab boy who liked me and who also lived in England. Poor Leela, if she did fall for Bruno, she was going to find it hard, because long-distance love and contact by emails wasn't the same as having a live boy to go to the movies with, hang out with after school and have regular snogging sessions with.

A middle-aged couple opened the front door and came out smiling. Both were tall and willowy, the man had a shock of white hair and was dressed in a fleece and cords and the woman had long, silver hair tied up at the back. She was very striking, with fabulous cheekbones, and must have been stunning when she was younger. She was dressed in a green kaftan top, jeans and had ropes of beads around her neck. Very bohemian. *Mum would love her,* I thought.

'Uncle Simon, Aunt Cora meet India Jane,' said Joe, after he and his mum had greeted them with hugs.

'Hi, welcome,' Cora said to me, then kissed both my cheeks.

We were bustled through the front door into a hall lined with paintings and into an airy kitchen at the back of the house which led to a sun room, which at first glance also served as a painting studio. I knew that Joe's uncle, Simon, was an artist so I was looking forward to seeing his work and talking to him about it.

They showed us our rooms: Joe's was on the first floor, and

mine was an attic room at the top. Once up there, I put my bag down on the patchwork eiderdown on the bed and looked around. The room had an old-fashioned feel – pale-pink wallpaper with sprigs of roses and leaves, lined dark-pink curtains and a window seat from where there was a stunning view of a terraced back garden which seemed to go on forever. On the one wall was a landscape watercolour and, on the other, a sepia photo of some people standing outside a mill. *Nice,* I thought.

I heard Cora call that tea was ready, so I slowly made my way back down the stairs to the kitchen. I loved the feel of the place, with its floor-to-ceiling shelves bulging with interesting-looking books on every floor, framed paintings, photos and drawings on all the walls, sculptures on various surfaces. I peeked into the living room, which was on the first floor. There were big squashy sofas next to a fireplace, a piano, more paintings and books. The kind of room I'd like to spend hours in. There was so much to look at and do on every floor that I wondered how we were going to fit in all the things to do in Bath, as well as properly investigating the house.

After tea in china cups and home-made scones and raspberry jam, Joe insisted that we went straight out to explore, so we grabbed our jackets, left Charlotte happily chatting with her brother and Cora, and set off down the hill into the town to explore.

Joe was the perfect guide and explained to me that Bath had begun as a Roman spa but was also famous for its Georgian architecture. 'It became the fashionable place for nobility and gentry to come to use the spa. In fact, we could go and use the baths ourselves.'

'Like proper toffs,' I said in my best Queen's voice.

'Exactly,' said Joe. He pointed to the opposite hill. 'Look, can you see that semi-circle of town houses over there? That's the Royal Crescent. Poshest address in Bath apparently, although where Uncle Simon lives is good, too.'

As we walked down the hill, I looked at the houses lining the street. All of them looked old, built from the honey-coloured stone typical of the area, some with wrought-iron verandas, others with little balconies, all with terraced gardens which would have stunning views of the hills on the opposite side.

Once in town, we had a walk around the centre, taking in the shops, the main square and the cathedral. In a lane behind one of the squares, we had hot chocolates in a tea shop called Sally Lunn's, which Joe told me was famous for its buns. Then we made our way over to the old Roman Baths, where we paid our money and joined the crowd of tourists who were making their way around.

'This is like taking a step back in time,' I said, as we followed the tourist trail up to an ancient-looking terrace lined with statues of Roman soldiers, then back down into the temple and a courtyard, then the centre part called the Great Bath Room where a large pool was full of steaming spa water which looked a strange green colour. After that, we went on to what was left of the changing room and then into what was the sauna in days gone by. It felt claustrophobic and damp in there with a musty smell, a bit like the bathroom at our new house until Mum and Dad transformed it. A guide was telling a group of Japanese tourists that going to the baths used to be a social outing, and I could just imagine it full of people hanging out and chatting in the same way that there were people from all nations around the Great Bath area today, sitting on the worn-down stones around the pool in their groups, taking photos, gazing at the artefacts and drinking in the atmosphere. Most of the rooms we went through were in ruins, a pillar here, half a wall there, part of a mosaic floor somewhere else, but there were lots of photos, drawings and miniature models to show exactly how it would have been laid out in the old days.

After the Baths, we walked up to the fashion museum, where we trawled the corridors looking at clothes from different eras. In one section, they had a sample crinoline skirt for people to try on and, of course, Joe had to have a go, so I took a picture of him in the full skirt and tight corset. He looked hilarious and a group of Italian tourists came through and started laughing and pointing and taking pictures of him, as if he was part of the exhibition. I couldn't stop laughing because, instead of being embarrassed, Joe got into it and posed for them. He even put a bonnet on and let them take a photo of him in that.

'I'll publish that on the school website,' I threatened, after the tourists had moved on.

He shrugged. 'Go ahead. I don't care. It will only show that I am in touch with my feminine side.'

I laughed. I thought it was cool that he didn't care what people thought.

The rest of the afternoon, we did the market stalls lining the main street, then walked to the bridge where there were more shops. Just around the corner from there, we could look down over the river and Joe took some photos of the water and the view of the bridge from there.

'There's only one other bridge in the world that has shops on it like Bath,' said Joe, after he fired off several shots of the boats waiting to take tourists down the river, 'and that's in Florence.'

'I know, the Ponte Vecchio. I have been there.'

Joe kissed my nose. 'Miss World Traveller,' he said.

'That's me. But I think I would like to come and live here some time,' I said. 'Maybe even study here.'

'Me too,' said Joe. 'The place is always buzzing. It's cool if you drive out, too. There are some awesome walks. I used to go with my uncle when I was younger.'

We held hands and walked back up the hill to the house where we had a chicken supper with Simon, Charlotte and Cora and when, later that night, I nestled down in my attic room, I decided that I would put Bath on my list of places to live, maybe even try and persuade Mum and Dad to move there one day.

★ ★ ★

Our second day, we got up early and, after a breakfast of fresh croissants, we set off straight down the hill to do a boat ride that we had seen advertised the day before. Down on the river, we boarded the boat and took seats on a bench on the upper deck. It was a bright sunny day, so we both got out our sunglasses and rolled up our sleeves to feel the sun on our skin. The boat soon filled up, we set off and it was lovely to see a different view of Bath from the water. As we floated along, we soon left the tall houses of the city behind and travelled through trees, fields and under bridges. Joe and I held hands and everything was exactly how I had hoped it would be, and I thought I would remember it for ever as one of my best romantic times. The boat ride took about an hour there and back and, by the time we returned, we were starving. On the bridge, we bought fresh orange and carrot juices, then hit the lanes again, where we bought big, sludgy yummy slices of pizza. *It really doesn't get any better,* I thought as I watched Joe tuck in with relish. We bought each other an Easter egg, then spent the rest of the afternoon cruising the shops in the lanes, where I bought ropes of beads to take back for the girls and postcards to send to Mum, Dad and Dylan.

'What are you going to write?' asked Joe, when we found a bench in the square where we sat and I got out my pen.

'Don't know. Um, the usual, *Weather is lovely, wish you were here?*'

'Nah. Too boring. Write: *Weather is here, wish you were lovely.*'

'Brill,' I said and began to write. 'Dylan will love that. And oh, it's your mum's birthday next week. Have you got her a card?'

'How do you know that it's her birthday?' asked Joe.

'Last time she was round at Aunt Sarah's, she told your mum that she was going to buy theatre tickets for her as a treat and, when I asked when the date was, she said just after Easter.'

Joe stiffened. 'You don't have to remind me,' he said, and he looked slightly annoyed.

'Oh, sorry. It's just coming from a family with brothers, they are all so rubbish at remembering birthdays. I always have to remind them.'

Joe stood up. 'Yeah, well no need to put me into the same category. You don't have to nag me. I always remember my mum's birthday.'

I felt hurt. The last thing I wanted to be was a nag. I got up and we began to walk back towards the house and, in the strange silence that had come down on us, my hurt turned to feeling cross.

'I was only trying to be helpful,' I said.

'About what?' asked Joe.

'About your mum's birthday.'

'You still on about that? Give me a break.'

His reaction surprised me. 'I wasn't *on* about it. I was only . . . oh never mind.'

'No need to get upset.'

'I'm not. I . . . oh forget it. I wish I hadn't brought it up.' I was beginning to feel tense though. Maybe he was right. I was getting upset. Had I been nagging him? I felt confused.

Suddenly I got the urge to push Joe in the river. Luckily for him, I managed to surpress it, but I really hate it when someone doesn't understand where I am coming from. I'd been trying to be helpful. We walked back up the hill in a frosty silence and I couldn't help but wonder what the heckity hoolah had happened.

The next day, the dark cloud that had descended over us had lifted and, after another breakfast of hot croissants and Cora's home-made raspberry jam, we spent the morning hanging around the house eating our Easter eggs, and looking at the many art books and at Simon's paintings. They were mainly watercolour landscapes of the area and were really good.

After a lunch of soup and fresh crusty bread, Simon drove us out to the country in his battered old BMW and we went for a long walk.

'Sorry about yesterday,' said Joe, after we had escaped the grown-ups and were walking ahead of them along the river in the sunshine.

'Me too,' I said. 'I think we were both tired.'

Joe nodded, took my hand and gave me a quick kiss.

We wandered on but both of us were quieter than usual. *I wonder if he's having doubts about me now that he's spent more time with me than usual?* I asked myself.

When we got back to the house, I was hoping that Joe and I would go down into town to explore a little more, there were so many places I still wanted to see, but Joe wanted to watch the football on telly. It had started to rain and I didn't want to go off on my own, so I went up to the lovely honey-coloured living room where I fell asleep on the sofa whilst looking at an enormous book about Picasso. I had my study books upstairs waiting for me, but the ones in the living room looked more interesting. Cora insisted that we stayed in for the evening and sent out for an Indian takeaway, then we watched a hysterical film called *Withnail and I,* which was about two mad actors and their trip to the country. Simon told me that it was his all-time favourite movie and that he had watched it about twenty times, and I did enjoy it but, if I had been given the choice, I would have gone out somewhere. It seemed a waste to be in watching a movie that I could see anytime when there was a whole new place to explore at the bottom of the hill, never mind a chance to spend more time alone with Joe.

Charlotte, Simon and Cora went up to bed around eleven and I thought that Joe and I might have a cosy half-hour snuggled up on the sofa. *Bliss,* I thought. However, after five minutes, Joe asked if I minded if he put the sports channel on. I said I didn't mind at all, thinking that we could still snuggle up, but Joe fell asleep. *So much for us having a romantic sesh,* I thought, as I watched him as he softly snored, his right arm up over his head, his hair tousled. *Is this what it's like in a long-term relationship? Some days you just don't gel, you have little to say to each other and it feels a bit flat?* The trip hadn't worked out the way I

127

had imagined and I hadn't done any studying either. I felt guilty about not doing any work and slightly peeved that I hadn't had more special moments like the one on the boat with Joe. *Oh don't be such a misery,* I told myself as I remembered one of Dad's favourite sayings: Blessed is he who has no expectations, for he is not disappointed.

I got out my phone to text Brook, Leela, Zahrah and Erin. I had promised that I would give them regular updates but, apart from a quick message when we had arrived and one from the boat, I hadn't been in touch and nor had they, apart from a quickie from Leela saying she was studying and it was raining. I felt the need to talk things over with one of them now and hoped someone might still be up and might even phone me for a girlie chat.

Anyone up? I texted. *SOS from Bath.*

I sent that off to the four of them, then realised that it might sound like I was in trouble. I quickly wrote another one:

Nthng urgnt. Just need to talk to a mate.

I had just sent it off and was wondering whether to wake Joe and tell him to go to bed, when I heard the doorbell ring. I waited a moment to see if Joe was going to stir or if there was any movement coming from Simon or Cora's room. All was quiet. The doorbell rang again, so I got up and went to see who was there.

I put the chain on the door before I opened it, then peeked through the gap.

'Who's there?' I asked.

A boy of about eighteen was standing on the porch. An exceptionally beautiful boy, not just handsome, this boy was in a league of his own, with shoulder-length hair and cheekbones to die for.

'I'm Finn,' he said. 'Son of —'

'Ohmigod. Cora and Simon,' I said. 'I'm, er . . . India Jane, guest. Er, don't you have a key?'

Finn nodded. 'Lost them. Drives Ma mad. You going to let me in?'

I realised that I still had the chain on the door so I quickly unhooked it, opened the door and stood aside to let Finn in.

He stepped into the hall, put out his hand for me to shake, looked into my eyes and, as I looked back, I felt a bolt of electricity.

'*Very* pleased to meet you, India Jane,' he said as I shook his hand. He didn't look away and held my gaze a while longer.

Wo-ah, a hubba hubba, I thought, as I felt my cheeks turn red.

Chapter 16

Boys, Boys . . .
and More Boys

I am the worst person in the world, I thought, as Finn caught my eye over the breakfast table and, as he had last night, held my gaze that moment too long, that moment that says, there's some chemistry going on here.

Cora came in from the studio at the back, saw her son and her face lit up. 'Ah, so you're back.'

'Last night,' he said and got up to hug her. 'Didn't want to wake you.'

'Have you met our guest?' Cora asked. 'Finn, this is India Jane Ruspoli. She's here with Joe.'

Finn glanced over at me. 'Indeed. Lucky Joe.'

'I . . . oh . . . yes,' I muttered. 'We met.' Why hadn't he said that we had met last night and spent a good half-hour chatting in the kitchen whilst everyone slept on the floors above us? He had been charming and made me feel like I was great company; he laughed at all my pathetic attempts at jokes and asked loads of questions about my life as if he really wanted to know.

Moments later, Simon and Joe came down and greeted Finn before tucking into breakfast. Finn looked across at me at one point and winked, and the croissant I was eating felt like glue in my mouth. I found the whole situation uncomfortable. I was sure it was written in neon lights on my forehead. *India Jane fancies Finn.* I tried to act casual and normal while he and Joe caught up, but I was sure that Finn was aware of the effect he was having on me because, for one thing, I blushed every time he caught my eye and, in return, his expression was one of amusement like we were sharing a good secret.

After breakfast, Charlotte wanted to get going on the journey back so it wasn't long before we had packed the car and said our goodbyes. Finn came out to see us off with his mum and dad and, while Joe was putting the last bag in the boot, Finn whispered that he hoped that we would meet up again sometime. I blurted something non-committal about loving Bath and hoping to come down with my family.

'What did you think of the beautiful Finn?' asked Charlotte, as she headed along the A4 out of Bath.

'Er . . . yes, he, um, seemed very nice,' I said, as I looked out at the rain that had started up. Nice was an understatement. I couldn't get him out of my mind – his wide smiling mouth, the denim-blue eyes, his perfect heart-shaped face.

'He *is* nice,' she said. 'So good-looking, isn't he? He's always getting scouts from modelling agencies stopping and begging him to join their books. His one flaw though is when it comes to girls. Isn't that right, Joe?'

Joe just laughed.

'Why's that then?' I asked.

'Oh, he knows he's gorgeous and he uses it to great effect. He has been known to play around with girls' hearts,' Charlotte replied. 'Cora is always having to console weeping girls who phone or turn up only to find that he has moved on.'

'Yeah. He's in a league of his own when it comes to girls,' said Joe. 'Don't get me wrong, he's a great bloke but he can be a tad ruthless. I've seen it, he likes to make the conquest then he gets bored.'

Thank God, I didn't do or say anything to give away how I felt, apart from blushing, I thought. *I would have looked so foolish and would have been just another girl on a long list.*

For the rest of the journey, I gave myself a telling off. First Tyler, then Bruno and now Finn. He kept popping into my mind but I told myself to blot him out. He was a non-starter. Not only did I have a boyfriend, but Finn was Joe's cousin and he was a player. He'd have made mincemeat out of me. *What is wrong with me?* I asked myself. I had the loveliest boyfriend so why did I keep fancying other boys? *Slut,* said a voice in my head. *I am so not a slut,* I argued back, but I did spend the rest of the journey wondering why I kept looking at other boys when I should have been happy with the one I had. *I am soooo not ever going to look at another boy ever ever,* I told both the voices in my head. *I am going to be a one-boy girl. That's me. Faithful. Focused. Not Finn's.*

'We've invited our neighbours for a late lunch,' said Mum, after Charlotte and Joe had dropped me home. 'They'll be here in half an hour. James and Clara, they're from the Caribbean so we will have plenty to talk about.'

'Shame about the rain,' said Dad as he looked out of the window. 'We'll have to eat in the kitchen.'

'But I have a ton of work to catch up on,' I said. 'I took it to Bath but didn't look at my books once.'

Dad put his arm around me. 'Ah, but you have been having experiences. The school of life – you can't beat it! There will be time later for your homework. I insist, first we eat, later you study. Getting along with neighbours is all part of moving to a new area, building good relationships.'

He wouldn't take no for an answer and I was given instructions to set the table. I put on the bright red-and-white gingham tablecloth, cutlery and napkins and went out on to the patio to see if the heavy clouds showed any signs of blowing over. Like the house, the back garden had been transformed.

Dad had borrowed a lawnmower from the neighbours on the right-hand side and the lawn, although patchy, was now neat and tidy, the furniture that had been dumped there and in the front was long gone. Mum and Dylan had been busy planting pots full of tulips and already they were showing a riot of red, yellow and pink flowers. Sadly the rain showed no sign of letting up, so I went back inside where Dad was busy cooking up one of his famous risottos and the kitchen smelled delicious, of onions, garlic and herbs.

'Can you get that?' asked Dad when we heard the doorbell ring.

I went to answer the door to find a dark-skinned couple about the same age as Mum and Dad standing there with a bunch of flowers and a bottle of wine. Despite the rain, under an umbrella, the man was wearing a bright Hawaiian shirt with parrots and leaves on it and the woman had a canary-yellow sundress on, both were tall and slender and looked like they could be fun. I introduced myself and invited them in.

'The twins are right behind us,' said James.

'Great,' I said, 'we have twins in our family, too.'

I led James and Clara through and Mum and Dad made them welcome so, when the doorbell rang again, I went to answer. Standing at the front door was a handsome black boy. He looked about Joe's age – tall, fit and dressed in jeans and a grey T-shirt.

'Oh hi,' I said. 'Er . . .'

'I'm Karl, er . . . we're invited for lunch?'

I nodded and beckoned him in. 'I thought there were two of you? Twins?'

Karl nodded and, at that moment, another boy appeared at the gate and waved. He was Karl's double and every bit as handsome.

'Marcus,' said Karl.

Two of them. Absolutely drop-dead gorgeous. I couldn't help it. I started laughing. The boys looked taken aback.

'What's so funny?' asked Karl.

'Nothing, no, come in, go through.'

'Not until you tell us why you're laughing,' said Marcus.

'Sorry. I don't mean to be rude. I was expecting . . . I don't know what I was expecting. Younger twins, I don't know why. Maybe because my nieces are twins. Younger. Girls. Silly really. Er . . . not as good-looking.' I realised that I was babbling. 'Yes. Sorry. Um. Do you ever feel like God is having a joke with you?'

The boys looked at me as though I was mad and then at each other.

'How come I haven't seen you about?' I asked.

'Uni,' said Marcus. 'I'm at Manchester, Karl's at Exeter. Home for the break.'

'Course. Why didn't I think of that? Um. Yes. OK,' I said. 'Go through. Out the back. Be with you in a mo. I just have to send an email.'

I raced upstairs to email Leela, Zahrah, Brook and Erin.

135

Boys. Boys. And more boys. Handsome boys. Can't stop laughing. Had made promise to self not to ever look at another boy except Joe but they keep on coming. In waves. Twins even. God is having a laugh with me. Help!

Five minutes later, I got an email back from Erin:

Get yourself on MSN now.

I went to MSN where she was waiting for me.

Irishbrat4eva: Oi you! Never mind boys, although I want to hear everything. Of course. But what about ME! You have been neglecting me something rotten. I haven't heard from you for ages.

Cinnamongirl: Excooth me. Nor me you. YOU have been neglecting me.

Irishbrat4eva: Haven't.

Cinnamongirl: Have. I texted you from Bath.

Irishbrat4eva: Big deal. Look, I know I haven't been in touch but I have been studying. That's all I do. No social life. No MSN. Mum has limited my time on the computer and she keeps checking up on me and if I dare to be doing anything that isn't study, like chatting to a mate, she gives me such a hard time. Thank God she's out at the mo.

Cinnamongirl: Ditto. Work, work, work, but you are still my bestest dearest friend forever.

Irishbrat4eva: Honest? Because I thought that maybe now you have moved on, new mates, new boyfriend.

Cinnamongirl: Never. Mates always come first. And you are my bestie.

Irishbrat4eva: Good. Now we have got that out of the way. Who are all these boys and when can I meet them?

Chapter 17

Back to School

'India Jane Ruspoli,' said Wendy Cadman, a prefect in the Sixth Form. I was waiting to see Mrs Goldman for our start of term assessment. Part of me was dreading it.

I knocked on the door.

'Come,' said Mrs Goldman.

I went inside and she indicated that I should sit down. She glanced at her papers then looked up. I felt nervous.

'How are you doing, India Jane?' she asked.

'Good. Um. I am trying to keep up. I know maybe . . .'

Mrs Goldman looked back at her papers and shook her head. 'I have been looking over your progress, India Jane.' She paused. 'Not good, India Jane, I am sorry to say. Not good.'

The knot in my stomach tightened. 'I have been working, honestly I have. And —'

Mrs Goldman held up her hand as if to quieten me. 'It's not a question of us doubting that. All the staff agree, you're bright, you're making an effort but it's just not enough, India. As you know, study leave starts soon for last exams, but I wonder if it's going to be enough. You're not going to get through.'

I felt like I was going to cry. 'I don't know what else to do, unless I stay up all night.'

'I am going to make a suggestion and that is that you do less not more.'

'Less?' A feeling of dread hit. *Please don't say I have to repeat the year,* I prayed.

Mrs Goldman nodded. 'There are a few subjects that you should be strong in, but they are suffering because I think you are spreading yourself too thinly. I am going to suggest that you drop a couple.'

'Drop?'

'History and music.'

'But . . .'

'Your coursework has to be in at the beginning of May then, as you know, lessons stop apart from science, so that everyone can concentrate on revising and practising for orals, in your case in French. The staff have talked it over and I think your best chance is if you focus on eight subjects, not ten.'

'But everyone else is doing ten.'

'And everyone else has been here since the beginning of the syllabuses. If you want to go ahead and do the ten, India Jane, then I won't stop you but I fear that, on what I have seen so far, you will get ten mediocre results and possibly even fail in some subjects, which is why I have suggested that you let go, focus your efforts, and get eight good results instead of ten weak ones. What do you say?'

I didn't have to think about it very long. Just the idea of it made me feel lighter. 'I think that's a great idea. Course I'll have to check with Mum and Dad but —'

'I think they will see the wisdom of it. Would you like me to speak to them?'

I nodded, but I already knew what they'd say and that was yes. They were both always on about not overdoing it and getting a balance in my life.

I left Mrs Goldman's office feeling like a weight had lifted. It was still going to be hard work but, somehow, now it felt more like a challenge than a losing battle.

'Options,' said Zahrah. 'That's what it's about.'

'Are you talking about boys or school?' I asked as I joined Brook, Leela and Zahrah, who were sitting on a bench outside the library enjoying the good weather that had arrived as soon as we had started back after the holidays.

'School,' said Zahrah. 'How did it go with Goldman?'

I filled them in on her suggestions and they all agreed that I should indeed drop two subjects. The more I thought about it, the more I liked the idea because history and music were my worst subjects.

Later that night, the word 'options' kept playing in my head, over and over. Options, options, boys, subjects, boys, subjects. I quickly texted Erin and asked her to go to MSN. She texted back that she would.

Irishbrat4eva: What's up, Brit girl?

Cinnamongirl: Am going mad.

Irishbrat4eva: Nothing new there then.

Cinnamongirl: Cheek. I don't know, Erin. I don't know what I want to do for a career. I don't know if I want to be in a relationship. I don't know nothing.

Irishbrat4eva: Ah. Then embrace the not knowing?

Cinnamongirl: Huh?

Irishbrat4eva: It's OK not to know. I think it happens sometimes that you hit a crossroads and don't know what to do. No harm in waiting until things become clear. Has something happened with Joe?

Cinnamongirl: No. We get on great. Bath was fab or at least most of it was. I keep beating myself up for all sorts of things. Fancying other boys. Feeling stuck with Joe sometimes. There I said it, I do feel stuck some days. But I love him, too. And I still don't know what I want to do when I leave school.

Irishbrat4eva: Have you met even more boys?

Cinnamongirl: No, just the boy in Bath and Bruno and I still like Tyler and the neighbours I told you about, Karl and Marcus. They're fun. Karl is a real clown when you get to know him and Marcus is so easy to talk to – and of course they will have mates. So many boys I like. But I feel bad about it. Bad, bad, bad. Guilty because I have a boyfriend.

Irishbrat4eva: Listen, just because you have a steady boyfriend, it doesn't mean that you become blind and deaf to the rest of the world. There will always be other boys. You're only human. You have to decide what you want though – to be free to explore said other boys or to cruise along with your boyfriend and accept that you're not available at the moment. Isn't Joe going away though?

Cinnamongirl: Gap year. Yeah. Think so. He wants to.

Irishbrat4eva: Hmm. So you have to decide how you're both going to handle that. And, as for not knowing what you want to do, chill. You have time. Even people who are clear about what they want to do for their careers change their minds sometimes. Options, Brit girl, give yourself options.

Cinnamongirl: You read my mind.

Irishbrat4eva: Begorah. Listen got to go. Time for beddybyes, speak soon.

Cinnamongirl: Thanks, agony aunt Erin.

Irishbrat4eva: You're welcome. Nightie night.

The next morning, after the best night's sleep I'd had in ages, I knew what I had to do.

I wrote a text to Joe in the school break. *Please meet me after school. India Jane X.*

He was waiting for me in our usual place at the wall opposite the gates and we went to Starbucks. On the way, I told him about dropping the subjects.

'Cool,' he said, 'but is that all you wanted to say?'

I shook my head. 'Not really. I . . . I have been thinking about my options. Zahrah said it yesterday and I realised that I really do want some – in my life, in my work. As you know, I've been finding it hard to decide what career I want to pursue. It's been bugging and bugging me and, yesterday, it was like I had this breakthrough.'

'So what have you decided?' he asked, when we got to the café and went to bag our favourite sofa by the window.

'Options. I've decided that I want options. That's why the word kept playing in my head. See, I still don't know what I want to be, maybe a tour guide, maybe an artist, maybe an interior decorator, maybe even a relationship counsellor.'

Joe cracked up.

'What's so funny?' I asked.

143

'No. Nothing. Relationship counsellor. Why not?'

I slapped his arm playfully. 'I have learned a lot in the last few months with you. A *lot*.'

Joe smiled and raised an eyebrow. 'Most girls do.'

'Big-head. But . . . I also, I don't know how to put this. I —'

'You want to break up?'

'No. NO. Well, actually . . . yes, sort of.'

I scrutinised his face for his reaction. He didn't seem freaked out by what I had said.

'Which is it?' he asked.

'Both. Ish. I've been thinking about it. A lot. I want options when I'm older. I want to be able to choose my career and in order to do that I have to get good grades. Up until now I have felt like I have been swimming against the tide, desperately trying to keep up but, yesterday, it was like Mrs Goldman threw me a lifeline.'

Joe nodded. 'Makes sense.'

'I think I can do it now. I really do, but it means that the next few months are going to be major, no distractions.'

Joe nodded again. 'I get it,' he said and pointed to himself. 'Distraction.'

I nodded and then Joe pointed at me. 'Also distraction.'

'So you understand?'

'I do,' he said. 'It's an important time in both of our lives and we can either go for it or not. I get what you're saying. I want those options, too. I don't want to be stuck, ever, in some boring job because I don't have any other choice. So yeah, India J. I get you.'

I sighed a breath of relief. 'So not breaking up . . .'

'As much as taking a break.'

'Exactly.'

'And when shall we resume?' asked Joe.

I grinned. 'Um. We could leave that open maybe?'

Joe nodded slowly as if considering what I was proposing. 'Like give ourselves options on that, too.' He put his arm around me and took a deep breath as if taking it in. 'This proves exactly why we are so right together. To be honest, I had been thinking along exactly the same lines but didn't know how to put it and, also, I wasn't totally sure I could do it. But you're right. We need to get our heads down so . . . yeah, this is great, take a break because you know I would never hurt you —'

'And I would never hurt you.'

'But if we agree, there won't be any bad feeling or guilt?'

I shook my head. 'Mutual agreement.'

'But we can maybe go on a date every now and then, yeah?'

I nodded. 'Sure. That would be lovely. And such a treat. But what about over the summer?'

'I wanted to talk to you about that. Sam and I have firmed up our travel arrangements. I was going to tell you this weekend – we aim to be gone a week after the exams.'

'So soon?' The thought of Joe not being there made me sad and I wondered if I was mad suggesting what I was. 'I will miss you.'

'And I you – but listen, hey, options. I know I am your first proper relationship, your first real love,' he said with a grin.

'Yeah, yeah big-head.'

'So listen I J, although one part of me finds this hard and, me being your first true love, you will be finding it hard, too.'

'Don't joke. I do actually,' I said and slipped my hand into his.

Joe squeezed it and the moment felt tender. He *was* my first love. *Am I insane?* I asked myself, as he looked deeply into my eyes and I felt I might cry.

'OK, India Jane. I agree. I think I have to let you go, for a short time anyway.'

I knew that now was the time to be totally honest. To be really clear. 'What about dating other people?' I asked. 'I mean, you will be away and you'll meet people, girls and I —'

Joe shrugged. 'It's only fair. Like, I can't expect you to hide yourself away while I trek around the world.'

'Nor me you,' I said. 'But that doesn't mean I won't get jealous but I . . . think it would be mean to say you must never kiss another girl or flirt or enjoy your time away.'

'Better to be honest and up front than cheat and lie and pretend something else is going on.'

'Exactly.' I thought about Finn and Karl and Marcus and Bruno and Tyler. 'That's what I want to be. It has been great with you, you know that, we have had such great times . . .' My words faltered and I felt like I was going to cry again. Joe squeezed my hand and stroked the back of it with his other

146

hand. 'But it's like it has all happened too fast. I don't think I am ready. I think I am too young to be in a proper relationship. All that stuff you said to me last summer. I know how you felt now. You meet people. You like them. You don't want to hurt anyone or lead them on or mess them around. Now I understand better why you were reluctant to commit.'

Joe nodded. 'So options, hey?' he said. 'We give each other options. It's a good option.'

'Not breaking up.'

'But taking a break.'

'So friends?' I asked.

'Always,' said Joe. And then he kissed me in a way that said we were way more than friends.

Later that night when I was in bed, I had a good cry. Joe *was* my first love and I still loved him in a way and probably always would. It felt like the end of a lovely chapter in my life. Yes, I was excited that, after exams were over, I would have a whole summer free in front of me but I couldn't deny the sadness I was feeling. *Maybe this is part of growing up,* I thought as Posh and Becks cuddled up at the end of my bed, *letting go, moving on. It's not easy. Maybe this is often how it's going to feel. Bitter-sweet.*

Chapter 18

Summer Barbie

Much later, on the day of the GCSE results in August, we had a barbecue at our house. Dad had invited half the neighbourhood as well as family and friends, and there were about fifty of us in the back garden. It really did feel like party time: sausages sizzling, chicken and vegetables on the barbie, burgers being burned!

'India Jane, come quickly, Joe on the phone,' called Mum from the house. I had spoken to him the week before from Peru, after he had got his A-level results. He had got one B, one A and two A-stars and had a place to go to Bristol University the following year. His Uncle Simon said he could stay with them if he liked, because Finn had a place at

Imperial College and would be coming up to London so his room would be free in term-time. Hmm . . . Joe had said that he would think about it but would probably prefer to be in digs with fellow students in Bristol. Joe's mum Charlotte had offered Joe's room to Finn but, much the same as Joe, he said that he wanted to stay in digs too, and didn't want any family member cramping his style. I could just imagine the damage he was going to do to his female fellow students' hearts and determined that I wouldn't be one of them, although as my motto goes these days: Open heart, open mind, open options. I might meet up with him for a coffee.

'Hey Joe,' I said when Mum handed me the phone. 'Are you in Mexico now?'

'I am and it's amazing. I'll put some pics up on Facebook.'

'Cool.' He'd posted photos when he could and I felt less distant when I saw him larking around in various locations with Sam.

'So?' he asked.

I knew what he was asking. What were my results? I had been to school that morning with Zahrah, Leela and Brook to get them.

'Zahrah got eight A-stars, two As. Leela six As, three A-stars and one B. Brook one A-star, seven As and two Bs.'

'Brainy bunch but I know they all worked for it. And?'

'Three Bs, three As and – tadah – two A-stars in art and English. I know it's not as impressive as the others but —'

'Are you kidding? No, that's brilliant, India Jane! Well done, I wish I was there to celebrate with you but . . . it sounds like you're not alone anyway. What is that noise?'

'Oh Mum and Dad have invited a few friends over,' I said, as I looked out at the colourful crowd packed into the back garden. Dad had organised a limbo line and there was a queue of middle-aged men in Hawaiian shirts waiting to dance under a skipping rope being held by Dylan at one end and Lewis at the other, while Dad pranced about like an idiot shaking castanets and Mum followed him doing some weird hippie dance. Sometimes, I despair about my parents.

'Sounds like party time,' said Joe. 'Hey, by the way, Sam said to say hi to Brook.'

'I'll pass it on,' I said. I knew that they had been in touch on Facebook too, and Sam had said he would see her when he was back. He had even sent me a friendly message from Greece, where he and Joe went first to work in a bar and earn some travel money. In the meantime, Brook wasn't pining. I glanced out at the garden, where she was sitting on a bench with Tyler eating strawberries dipped in chocolate.

'How are the others?' asked Joe.

'Cool. Zahrah is still with Ryan.'

'And Leela?'

'I think she's got her eye on one of the neighbours,' I said as I watched Leela, who was sitting on the grass on a rug between Karl and Marcus and looking like the cat that got the cream.

'And you?'

'Single. Keeping my options open. You?'

'Ditto,' he said, then laughed. 'See you at the end of August before we go off again, my option numero uno.'

'Ditto.'

When we'd finished our call, I put the phone down but it rang again immediately.

'Hey, it's me. Go to Skype,' said Erin's voice.

'Let me get the others,' I said, and I quickly whizzed around the garden to tell Zahrah, Leela and Brook to join me and together we raced up the stairs to the computer, switched to Skype and, a second later, there was Erin's pretty face staring out at us. Mum had got me a webcam for my birthday and Erin and I had been in regular contact over the last few weeks. It made the world feel like a smaller place and would be even smaller if Joe was ever in an Internet café some place that had one. I switched on the camera over the screen, so that Erin could see us too.

'Hey, it's the crew,' she beamed back, when she saw that we were all there.

'Hi, Erin,' we all chorused.

'When are you coming over?' asked Brook.

'Next week,' said Erin. 'Can't wait.'

'How did you do?' I asked.

'Two A-stars, four As, three Bs, one C.'

'Wow, that's fantastic, Erin,' I said, and we quickly told her our results.

She grinned back at us. 'Watch out world, hey? Now, how's that party going over there? Are you saving any boys for me?'

Leela did a thumbs-up. 'We have loads of boys for you to meet. A whole beauty parade to choose from. Apart from Ryan, of course, who is taken, but we have met tons of new people. We're young, we're single, wah-hey.'

'And we still have a few more days of blissful summer hols. Life doesn't get any better, does it?' said Erin.

After the call, I went back into the garden where Tyler had got me a plate of food, and Karl and Marcus had joined the queue for limbo along with a bunch of mates from their school. I sat on the rug and looked around. Erin was right. Life really didn't get any better. Joe would be back at some point but, in the meantime, we were still mates, still in touch. My family had a great place to live. I had my place in the Sixth Form and would at last be starting the syllabus with everyone else. But until then, I had options. Hmm. One of Dad's favourite songs was playing on the CD player. 'Expecting to Fly' by Buffalo Springfield.

That's me, I thought as I listened to the lyrics. *I'm standing on the edge of my future, feeling like I could soar above the clouds. Expecting to fly.*

If you've enjoyed Cinnamon Girl,
try these other series by Cathy Hopkins!

Mates, Dates

Four friends and one fab rollercoaster ride as they
go through the ups and downs of teen life.

The MATES, DATES series

Companion Books:

What would you do if you had to tell the complete **truth** for a day? Would you **dare** enter a national singing competition? Could you cope with what happens when you **kiss** the school heart-throb? Could you **promise** to be faithful, whatever form temptation takes?

Becca, Cat, Lia, Squidge and Mac all enjoy playing the *Truth, Dare, Kiss or Promise* game to liven up their lives – but they can never predict where it's going to lead them!

The TRUTH, DARE, KISS, PROMISE series

www.cathyhopkins.com

Like this book?
Become a mate today!

Join CATHY'S CLUB and be the first to get the lowdown on the LATEST NEWS, BOOKS and FAB COMPETITIONS straight to your mobile and e-mail.

PLUS there's a FREE MOBILE WALLPAPER when you sign up! What are you waiting for?

Simply text MATE plus your date of birth (ddmmyyyy) to 60022 now! Or go to www.cathyhopkins.com and sign up online.

Once you've signed up keep your eyes peeled for exclusive chapter previews, cool downloads, freebies and heaps more fun stuff all coming your way.

What would you do if you had to tell the complete **truth** for a day? Would you **dare** enter a national singing competition? Could you cope with what happens when you **kiss** the school heart-throb? Could you **promise** to be faithful, whatever form temptation takes?

Becca, Cat, Lia, Squidge and Mac all enjoy playing the *Truth, Dare, Kiss or Promise* game to liven up their lives – but they can never predict where it's going to lead them!

The TRUTH, DARE, KISS, PROMISE series